The Edge of Everywhen

The Edge of Everywhen

A.S. Mackey

B&H
PUBLISHING
NASHVILLE, TENNESSEE

Published by B&H Publishing Group
Nashville, Tennessee

Dewey Decimal Classification: JF
Subject Heading: CHANGE—FICTION / MYSTERY FICTION /
FAITH—FICTION

Cover illustration by Ross Dearsley

1 2 3 4 5 6 7 • 24 23 22 21 20

This book is dedicated to Tammy West,
my first Reader, and to every librarian in
small towns and big cities across the globe.
Your contribution to literacy is immeasurable.

Contents

Contents

Villa Legere

1st Floor

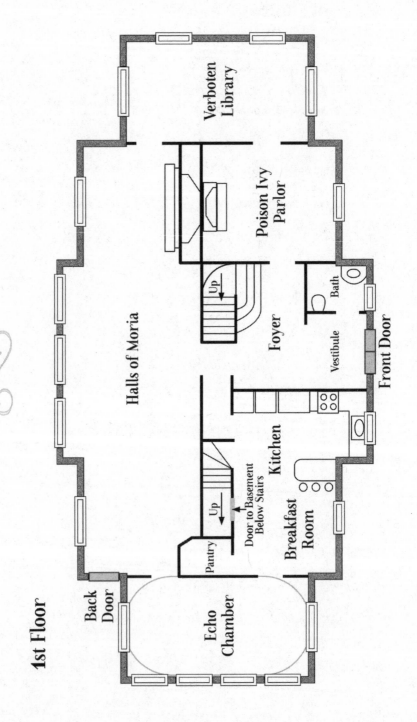

Verboten Library

Poison Ivy Parlor

Halls of Moria

Up

Foyer

Bath

Vestibule

Front Door

Kitchen

Up

Door to Basement Below Stairs

Pantry

Breakfast Room

Back Door

Echo Chamber

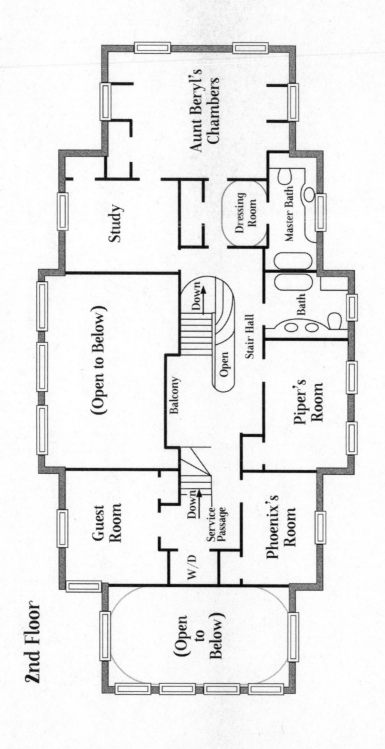

2nd Floor

Aunt Beryl's Chambers

Study

Dressing Room

Master Bath

Bath

(Open to Below)

Stair Hall

Down

Open

Balcony

Piper's Room

Guest Room

Down

Service Passage

W/D

Phoenix's Room

(Open to Below)

Salutations

May our stories be told,
and may the words have life.
−Friar Godfried

The day the girl and the boy showed up at my door was like any other. Their arrival is now etched into my spine and has become part of me, just as I have become part of them.

Just as I will become a part of *you*.

Do not worry, Dear Reader. You will become part of my existence, as all my Readers do, leaving chocolate bar smudges or chicken nugget fingerprints on a few pages before returning me to the library shelf. Just to let you know, I am rather averse to honey, because my pages get sticky. And milk can sour into an awful stench if it spills on the cover, but I really don't mind. I was created for *you*, Dear Reader.

You fascinate me.

Ah, I'm distracted from my tale; my apologies. Back to the somber children shivering at my door.

The pristine air of the library was lonely that morning, like much of the estate. Empty of Readers, empty of children. The arrival of two smallish humans was a breath of invigorating air, for I had grown musty of late.

The frigid wind pressed hard against the outside walls that afternoon. Can you feel it? Wafting from my spine and over the pages of Chapter One, misty vapors curl up to chill your glove-less fingers grasping my cover, vapors that send a shiver down into your slippers. Perhaps you should fetch a blanket for this part. Careful with the cocoa. Marshmallows can be worse than honey if they escape the mug and dribble, sticky, down the side.

That morning some of the frost demanded to be let in through the gypsum and twelve decades of paint and wallpaper. Icy pools of air curled in the hollow spaces near the corners of the library, and the costly Persian rugs looked warm down there on the floor.

Quite a pair, those two. Piper and Phoenix.

What's that?

Well, I couldn't *see* them, Dear Reader. I don't have eyes as you do. But I did see them. I *perceived* them as they stood by the porch. I could feel the heavy thrum of Piper Guthrie's sullen heart as she stood at the door clutching her bravery like a stone in her stomach. Her heart had been ticking for thirteen roller-coaster years, and now it was tough and bruised around the edges, like the heart of the kid picked last for dodgeball six years in a row.

I sensed the birdlike chirp of her little brother's inner clock as well. The one and only Phoenix Guthrie. His ten-year-old heart skipped and twittered, going through its instinctive motions as he stood and waited on the landing with his sister. He wondered again where their mother, Naomi, was, and whether she would be there with peanut butter on the other side of the door.

Peanut butter, straight from the jar. It was the boy's favorite food of all time, and he could have lived on nothing else.

Phoenix knew the presence of Piper. She was here, and he could see her and hold her hand on the rare occasions that he wanted to, like now. Her hand was soft and familiar while everything else around him was sharp, unknown, and bitterly cold. This imposing dwelling was nothing like the trim little cottage in not-as-cold Atlanta where Phoenix had lived from his birth until this raw April morning.

Phoenix missed the presence of his mother, Naomi. He felt her absence like an entire section of suddenly missing teeth, searching with his tongue for the solid mass that was once there and finding only empty craters still raw and in need of healing.

The ghost of a foggy reminder that used to be called Dad drifted in and out of the boy's thoughts as well. Every now and then a sand-covered memory would rise to the surface and then slip away.

The pictures in the boy's laminated flipbook showed these people all in order. His mother, Naomi; his father, Gordon; his sister, Piper; and Phoenix. *Phoenix.*

Who was Phoenix?

Who, indeed?

Phoenix knew who Phoenix was, but he couldn't always tell the people around him.

He began rocking back and forth from the waist as he held his sister's hand. The two children stared at the unfamiliar and massive door in front of them, a door so large that Piper wondered if Hagrid might be about to crash through from the other side.

Ah! Perhaps you didn't expect to see a reference to Hogwarts in my pages. Have you read any of the marvelous *Harry Potter* stories, Dear Reader? I would not be surprised if you had read every last one, and the companion books as well.

I sized up the children as Mr. Greene brought their suitcases inside and placed them on the spotless hardwood floor in the foyer. As they waited for instructions, both Piper and Phoenix allowed themselves a timid glance around the entrance of their new home. Shell-shocked into an angry silence, Piper gazed at the unfamiliarity of the ornate arched doorways and the vaulted ceilings and the polished woodwork glaring at her from every surface. The extravagant furnishings shouted, "Don't touch! Quiet! We do not like fingerprints or children!"

I breathed out their names in a whisper meant only for them.

Phoenix alone heard me. His heartbeat quickened as he looked in my direction through the open parlor doorway. If not for the firm hand of his sister, he would have come to get me from the shelf straight away. Electricity rippled through my spine with the assurance that I had found my next Reader.

Reading would have to wait, however. There was an Aunt Beryl to meet.

Oh! Forgive me; I have failed to introduce myself. My name is Novus Fabula. The pleasure is all mine, Dear Reader.

What's that you say? Books cannot speak?

On the contrary, Dear Reader. *Quite* the contrary. Books are one of the few things on this earth that truly speak, from the moment the first word is penned until the book's last Reader has drawn their final breath.

Let me show you.

2

A Tragedy Occurs

In the pages of a book she found truth, lies, mystery, wonder, and balm for the wounds she didn't know she carried.
—Novus Fabula

We must hit pause, Dear Reader, but only for a moment. Let us jump back in time a bit, and perhaps these events will make the children's arrival in this unfamiliar territory make more sense.

The deep cadence of Piper's jagged breaths echoed through her bedroom as she lay fast asleep. She was dreaming. Only the books stood watch, but of course they could do nothing. Those books were her dearest friends, but they remained a collection of ink on paper, bound in linen, imprisoned high on the shelf.

Something was covering Piper's eyes.

Something was covering her mouth as well, and she wanted to scream with her whole body, but she couldn't. Her lungs wanted air, *needed* air. It was like the time she had spent too long in the deep end of the big pool and her father had dragged her out of the water the third time she went under.

Molasses air. Heavy limbs. Every part of Piper's dream world was thick and moving in slow motion.

Phoenix and Piper floated on a sturdy yellow life raft. An inky blue-black night covered everything above and around them. The boy's clammy hand was vice-gripped to his sister's, and she found a measure of comfort in the familiar scent of peanut butter. As Phoenix rocked back and forth, the raft bobbed gently underneath the pair in response. The sky had begun to spit fat drops of ice-cold rain onto their heads, and Piper wondered how long it would be before the raft would fill up and sink.

Do I detect droplets of water splashing onto the edges of Chapter Two? Best if you approach these pages with a towel, Dear Reader. You may wish to keep a flashlight close by, in case the power flickers, and a raincoat may come in handy.

The children had set out on the raft with their mother looking for their father so long ago, and Piper wasn't sure what happened just before this part. Did Naomi fall out of the raft? Why didn't she call for help? Naomi, the strongest swimmer of them all, had taught Piper to swim in the ocean eight years ago.

No splash, though. Where was her mother? How long had she been gone?

Piper was startled by the faint aroma of a lavender and eucalyptus perfume passing on the breeze. It moved of its own free will, curling through Piper's hair and grazing the cheeks of both children. Piper turned toward the warm scent and breathed in deep, but the place in her chest where she usually felt her mother was an echoing, hollow cave. There was only the solid, silent presence of Phoenix rocking beside her. The children could hear waves of water lapping against the sides of the raft as thunder sounded off in the distance.

Phoenix became still and looked his sister directly in the eye, something he hadn't done since he was very little. No one knew where he got those eyes, eyes that drifted between green and gold depending on what mood he was in. Peace and calm flowed out from them now, telling his sister not to worry.

Worry was easy for Piper, easy as breathing and just as constant. Her father's construction company had sent him far away to help rebuild a destroyed school. It was hard enough having her father work overseas for three months at a time. But two years ago Gordon didn't show up at the worksite one day. All anyone could say was that he had been taken in the street by armed soldiers in a tan military truck, and no one could tell them why.

By now Piper was used to the weight of worry and used to the hardest part of it all—the Not Knowing.

A streak of lightning ruptured the black, followed by a cannon blast of thunder. The sudden explosion tore the dream-raft out from under the children, dumping them both onto Piper's real-life bed back on the wide-awake earth. A cotton blanket was tangled and wrapped all around Piper's face, and she sucked in air as she peeled off the sheets and sat up, drenched with sweat, heart pounding.

Phoenix was sitting on the edge of Piper's bed, silent and staring at the wall as he slowly rocked back and forth. An early March storm was howling in the dark just outside the bedroom window, and Piper took a few deep breaths as her heart rate slowed and she tried to let go of the dream.

Near her diary and the mountain of books tempting gravity on her nightstand, a note from Phoenix was propped up against the old electric clock radio her father had given her. Phoenix had left the note there for Piper some time before dinner several hours earlier, but Piper had buried her head in a book again and forgot about deciphering it. Her brother's little scribbled notes were written in a special number code, and it was the only way Phoenix ever talked to her.

Piper shared that secret with no one.

She took her brother's hand, curious as to why he had left his bed and come into her room in the middle of the night.

"You okay, kiddo?" she asked, even though she didn't expect him to answer. The mystery of autism had caused Phoenix to go silent years ago. His frustrated rocking episodes had become less frequent over the last several months though, thanks to the special school he'd started attending. His teacher said he was Making Progress.

Piper was wondering how long Phoenix had been sitting there when her bedroom door opened. She squinted and blinked toward a bright flood of light spilling in from the hallway.

"Are you awake, Piper?" It was Chelsi, the grad-school babysitter that stayed the night with Phoenix and Piper any time their mother had staff meetings at work that ran late. Chelsi sniffed and cleared her throat, her voice coming out in broken pieces of gravel.

"There's been an accident," she said. She walked stiff and zombie-like into the room and sank down on the edge of the bed. Chelsi's eyes were puffy and her cheeks were wet, her tears reflecting the glare from the hallway light as she stared at nothing.

The sudden dryness in Piper's throat made it impossible to swallow the lump that had risen there. Her heart skipped a beat as her thoughts returned to the yellow life raft in the Darkness Where Mom Was Not. Piper leaned back against the pillows, realizing that her little brother's grip had tightened on her hand to the point of pain. Phoenix's rocking became more pronounced as Piper asked Chelsi a question she wasn't sure she wanted answered.

"Where's my mom?"

This took place a month ago, Dear Reader.

And now you know the reason the children came to be standing in my foyer, and why I needed to tell them a story.

3

The Gloomy Coast

The day had simply been full of Too Much Muchness.
So Clarence hid between the covers of his favorite
storybook until the day should sort itself out again.
—Bartholomew Stout

Piper smoothed out the crumpled note Phoenix had just shoved into her hand.

160-4-10, 122-30-1, 6-20-5

Phoenix strained against the seatbelt as he rocked back and forth, staring at the back of the empty passenger seat in front of him and focusing on nothing. Beside him in the spacious back seat, Piper dug into the crumby bottom of her denim backpack on the floorboard and pulled out her tattered copy of the cipher key. *The Giver* was just one of a handful of books she had crammed into the backpack before leaving their Atlanta house at dawn that morning.

You've already plowed through *The Giver*, Dear Reader; correct? Did your language arts teacher assign it? Your librarian will be happy to secure a copy for you if it's one of the classics you missed.

Piper flipped through the dog-eared pages to find the corresponding words for each number to decipher the message. She wondered where Phoenix had managed to find paper or a pen in this brand new, stain-free, adults-only car.

His note said, "vehicle smell strange."

Piper's stomach twisted into a guilty knot when she realized she wasn't thinking about how scary all this newness must be for Phoenix. She had been thinking about her mother again, picturing a smile framed with freckled cheeks and thick sun-streaked hair in a ponytail. Piper tried and failed to find a place to stuff the ache in her chest. She'd been forcing herself to read *A Wrinkle in Time* for the last hour, but the words kept swimming away as she read the same paragraph six times. She thought about pulling out her diary, but she hadn't found the words she needed to say just yet.

Piper glanced up at the driver, a beanstalk of a man wearing a spotless charcoal suit and a matching forties-looking hat that brushed the ceiling of the car. The driver's eyes were riveted to the twisting, rain-soaked road, and the man had hardly said a word since meeting the children at the airport. Piper thought his face was nice though. Crinkling laugh lines branched out from the corners of his eyes, and he looked like Piper's favorite goofy math teacher who cracked dumb jokes to help her understand her fractions homework.

Piper nodded the tiniest bit in answer to her brother's message. She couldn't count the number of times their parents had asked her what Phoenix needed or wanted, because they couldn't pick up on his silent cues the way she could.

She checked her cell phone for the fourth time since leaving the Bangor airport.

SEARCHING FOR SERVICE . . .

Great. Now I can't even text Gabriella to tell her about the fancy-schmancy driver picking us up today.

They hadn't passed another car for miles, and Piper wondered if it would be rude to ask the driver how much farther it was to Aunt Beryl's house.

As she thought about the Unknown Aunt Beryl, Piper's body gave an involuntary shudder. Her imagination had conjured up plenty of witchy and warty images of a wiry-haired, frowning hag who may or may not eat small children and keep tarantulas as pets. Because their mother had died in the car crash a month ago, and their father had been missing for more than two years now, the papers at the bank had said that Aunt Beryl, their father's last living relative, had to take care of the children. Phoenix and Piper had met Aunt Beryl once, when Piper was three and Phoenix was a baby, and no one had remembered to bring a camera that day. The only photos of Aunt Beryl in their family albums were from when Gordon was just a year old and Beryl was newly married. That was a thousand years ago, and Piper envisioned that Aunt Beryl must be held together with dust by now.

Still staring at nothing and rocking back and forth, Phoenix reached toward Piper across the seat and grabbed his sister's hand. The scent of peanut butter, fresh from his customary snack that morning, lingered between them.

Piper was glad her brother was with her, and she couldn't imagine ever being separated from his quiet presence. But she still wished Gabriella was there in person so they could talk. The girls had been best friends since third grade, and Piper wanted someone who would answer back with words.

"Your brother cares a great deal about you," said the driver, startling Piper from her thoughts. "He doesn't say much though." The man kept his eyes on the road as he asked, "It's Phoenix, right?"

Piper nodded. "He doesn't talk," she said. "The doctors say he has autism. Do you know what that is?"

The driver's eyes softened as he looked in the rear-view mirror at his two young charges. "Yes, I do," he answered. "Means he learns and expresses himself differently than you and I." Piper had never heard her brother's autism referred to in such a simple, straightforward way.

"He isn't a freak, in case you wondered," Piper said. "He hasn't said anything out loud since he was six, but he's the smartest person I know. He reads a book once, and he's memorized it. He can write down the page number, the line number, and the position of every single word in the book. It's called being a savant."

The driver nodded. "That's quite an impressive gift," he said, and Piper was surprised that he actually seemed to mean it.

"So, what do we call you?" Piper blurted out. "I saw the name *Greene* on your metal name tag thingy when we got off the plane, but is that really your name? Just Greene?"

The driver's face creased into a giant smile as he responded. "Original Asher Greene, at your service," he announced with a dutiful nod. "Pleasure to know you both."

"Your first name is *Original!?*" Piper asked with a snort.

Naomi had always taught the children not to make fun of anything that seemed different, but lately Piper hadn't been all that concerned about being nice. *Original* was the strangest name she had ever heard.

"The one and only," he announced.

"I think I'll call you Mr. Greene, if that's okay," said Piper, trying hard not to crack a smile.

He nodded, still smiling. "Mr. Greene is just fine, young lady. It's Piper, isn't it? Or would you prefer that I call you Miss Guthrie?"

"Piper is good," she said. "'Miss Guthrie' sounds old lady-ish." Piper's bravery increased with Mr. Greene's normal-sounding conversation. "So, are you like my aunt's chauffer?" she asked.

Mr. Greene nodded and said, "One of the many hats I've worn for your aunt over the last thirty years is that of a driver. Officially, I'm the butler, graduate of the American Butler School in New York with a certification in estate management."

"Wow," she said. "That sounds so official and . . . involved."

Mr. Greene laughed. "*Involved* is the perfect word to describe what I do."

"Is there cell-phone service at my aunt's house?" Piper asked, glancing again at her still-searching phone with dwindling hopes.

"Sorry to say there is none," Mr. Greene replied. "You might be able to get a few bars of service in the town nearby, and they also have an internet café with computers that customers can use if you don't have a laptop. Your aunt has a landline with a dial-up modem, and a separate fax line. Does that help?"

Piper hoped her disappointment wasn't evident. "No problem," she lied. "Will I have my own room?" she asked. "Or will I share with Phoenix? It's okay if we share; we don't mind." Piper wouldn't have cared if the two of them were moving into a one-room wooden shack, because at least she and Phoenix were together, and they had somewhere to live with grown-ups who might shop for peanut butter. By the looks of Mr. Greene and his car and his hat and his butler-y speech, Piper figured they weren't going to end up in a one-room shack.

Mr. Greene nodded. "That's very accommodating of you, but the new housekeeper insisted that every teenage girl *must* have her own room." He smiled at the children through the rear-view mirror again. "You don't have to share unless you want to."

Piper nodded. "Okay. I guess we can let Phoenix decide. Taking him out of his routine has been really hard, so I'm not sure how he'll do with a new bed in a new house with a bunch of strangers who don't know what he needs."

What Piper *wanted* to say, Dear Reader, was that Phoenix needed his mother, and that all of this was wrong, and that she was ready to wake up from this weird nightmare.

For the thousandth time that day Piper reached out to Naomi in her thoughts, remembering as the pang hit her chest that her mother wasn't there. Piper pulled her diary and a pen from her backpack and began to scribble.

Dear Dad,

I used to write to Dear Diary but a diary's just a book filled with lines, and you're a real person, and since Mom isn't here, maybe you're still out there somewhere like she said. I don't know. Mom used to say never to give up hope about you, and Phoenix and I need you to come back NOW.

Getting a construction job was stupid.

And what if Aunt Beryl doesn't like me?

4

Laws of the Kingdom

*"It's been fifteen years since I read any
sort of book," he said with his nose in the air.
"Reading is so bothersome." Gracie rolled her
eyes and said, "Well that explains everything."*
—Johannah Whitney

Now we are back to the beginning again, Dear Reader. Sometimes it's a bit better when stories go round in a few turns instead of marching straight through in a boring line, don't you think?

Both children got out of the car into the bracing April air, and Piper shivered from a combination of nerves and a biting gust of wind as she stared at the largest, gloomiest house she had ever seen. She was glad for the heavy windbreaker Chelsi had suggested she bring, and she drew her arms in against a sudden chill.

Georgia was never this cold. I'm gonna need some long underwear.

Mr. Greene retrieved two small suitcases from the trunk. The children walked up the stone steps toward the arched timber door, and Piper half expected Lucy or Edmund Pevensie to come running around the corner of the house. (I just know you've heard of the *Narnia* tales, Dear Reader!) Naomi had always wanted to live in an English Tudor, so Piper knew what the style of house was called, but she had never seen one except in movies. It was sad and lovely, and she wondered why Aunt Beryl would live virtually alone in such a fortress.

Will she be glad that we've invaded her house, much less her whole life? Or will Phoenix and I get in her way? How many people have to live here before it doesn't feel empty?

The front door swung open, and three large blobs of fur and wagging tales exploded out the door and onto the porch. Mr. Greene laughed and said, "Ah, the welcoming committee of Villa Legere!"

"Dogs!" Piper exclaimed. "We've never had dogs before!"

The dogs bounced around Piper, sniffing and slobbering on her shoes and pant legs and backpack and ankles. Mr. Greene's expression became stern as he commanded, "Sit!" and all three dogs obeyed, sitting properly with barely contained excitement and lolling tongues.

"What's a villa leg thingy that you just said?" Piper asked.

"Oh. Villa Legere is the name your late uncle gave to the estate years ago when he and your aunt first bought it," Mr. Greene explained. "Depending on what language you translate it into, it means either 'estate of light' in French, or 'estate to read' in Latin."

"Huh," Piper said with a nod.

"The golden retriever is Lincoln," Mr. Greene said, patting each dog on the top of the head by way of introduction. "He's only a year old, so he's still got a few manners to learn. The Irish setter is Teddy; he's four. And the mastiff, the gray boss-man of the group here, is Quincy. He's ten." Mr. Greene leaned toward Piper with a smile and added, "Named after presidents."

"Is it okay to pet them?" Piper asked.

"Oh, yes," said Mr. Greene, closing the trunk of the car. "Your aunt sent the dogs to obedience school as puppies, so they obey commands and won't eat your homework or your broccoli unless you ask them to."

Piper stroked Lincoln's thick fur, amazed at how soft it was. The energetic retriever began licking Piper's hand, and the dog's sturdy tail thumped on the stone porch as Teddy edged in closer for a share in the petting. Then, as if on cue, all three dogs crowded around Phoenix and perched at his feet as if they had known him his entire life. The three canines looked up at the boy with doggie question marks on their faces, waiting for a command. Phoenix didn't openly acknowledge the trio as he stared at his feet, but his entire body became still as he allowed each dog to nuzzle his hand one at a time.

Mr. Greene raised his eyebrows with a surprised smile and said, "Interesting."

A plump middle-aged woman bustled outside and greeted the group with an enormous smile. "Original Greene, you get those freezing kids inside right this minute!" she said. She had tried to pin her unruly hair into some sort of bun, but twenty-seven stray and wiry gray curls had escaped the hairpins and were sticking out in different directions all over her head.

Piper was reminded of photos she'd seen of Albert Einstein, and she wondered if the woman was recovering from a recent electrocution. "Aunt Beryl?" Piper asked.

The woman doubled over laughing. "Oh, no, honey!" she said. As she tried in vain to re-pin a strand of hair behind one ear, she said, "I'm Ms. Bouchard's housekeeper, Sofia. You two hungry?"

Mr. Greene set the suitcases down inside the front door on spotless hardwood floors as the children came in and shrugged off their jackets. Piper looked at Phoenix, trying to remember the last time he had eaten something. "Yes, please," she replied. She was too nervous to be hungry, but she hoped that a snack would ease some of the awkwardness as they shuffled from the entryway into the foyer and into my sights.

I called Piper's name, but a simmering anger filled her ears with other noise and she couldn't hear me just yet. So I called her brother's name.

Phoenix.

The boy looked over his right shoulder through the parlor and into the library, his eyes finding me on the shelf within seconds.

Hello, Dearest Phoenix. I am honored to know you.

Phoenix turned and began to walk toward me, but Piper grabbed his hand, oblivious to the object of his interest. She was busy digesting the view of the cavernous entryway as she wondered what awaited them.

"Is Aunt Beryl here?" Piper asked, her voice going up to echo around the high ceilings.

"She's upstairs in the study," said Mr. Greene as he removed his hat and overcoat. He placed them on the wooden rack inside the door. "Your aunt spends her days working on grants and paperwork for different charity foundations, and I believe she's on the phone at the moment. She'll be down shortly, so if you'll follow Sofia to the kitchen, she's prepared a snack for you. I'll put your bags in your rooms and let your aunt know you've arrived."

Piper pictured her mother greeting long-lost relatives at the door with a plate of warm cookies and hugs all around.

Mom would never let someone else answer the door when she expected guests!

A graceful oak staircase curved up to the second floor from the foyer. Piper and Phoenix followed Sofia under the staircase through an arched doorway, where Sofia turned left to go down a hallway.

Piper sensed an echo beyond the next archway, a perception of space that felt large and open. She was far too curious to follow Sofia to the kitchen, so she walked forward through the archway and found herself in an immense ballroom.

Running left to right the full length of the house with ceilings in the center that soared thirty feet high, the ballroom was flooded with cold light from five enormous windows. Several tapestries depicting strolling lords and ladies hung on the walls, and each tapestry was so large it would have dwarfed her parents' king-sized bed. Piper noticed an oversized stone hearth down to her right on the inner wall, a hearth that opened into a fireplace big enough for both children to stand in, side by side. Piper smiled as an image of Frodo and Sam being chased by goblins through the dwarf hall beneath the mountain came to mind.

I will call this room the "Halls of Moria."

Should I mention that Mr. Tolkien was a friend of mine, Dear Reader? I'm quite the fan of Bilbo, Frodo, and Gandalf. I'm especially fond of Samwise Gamgee.

Phoenix followed his sister, looking beyond the air at nothing as he wandered around the huge room, all three dogs trailing along inches from his feet on the white floors. Piper wondered if any of the dogs had ever peed on the marble.

Sofia's gentle voice interrupted Piper's thoughts. "Ever seen a room this big?" she asked as she repositioned one of the useless hairpins on her head. "This is where Ms. Bouchard hosts her fund-raising shindig every spring and fall. Let's get that snack now, okay?"

Phoenix, Piper, and all three dogs obeyed, following Sofia down a hallway that ended in a bright and airy kitchen. Attached to the kitchen was a small breakfast room, and beyond that through an open doorway they could see the fancy curving woodwork of a formal dining room table.

A small tray of peanut butter and jelly sandwiches was sitting out on the breakfast bar along with a bowl of apples, bananas, pears, and oranges. Piper was surprised to see that the sandwiches were made with white bread with the crusts cut off. Piper would have pegged their new guardian as a high fiber, whole grain, eat-your-crust type of relation.

"Wait, how did you know that Phoenix likes peanut butter?" Piper asked, watching Phoenix take a seat on a barstool and begin munching on a sandwich. The dogs lay at his feet, their bodies surrounding the bottom of his chair like a doggie moat.

Sofia poured out two mugs of piping hot cocoa. "Mr. Greene did a whole lotta digging to find out everything about you both," she said. "Having snacks you like could make these first few days here a little easier, maybe?" She patted Piper's hand and leaned in to whisper. "I'm a newbie, too, if you didn't know. I started here three weeks ago, so we can all be new together. I stocked up on tons of peanut butter for Phoenix, and peppermint tea for you."

Piper bit into a banana and asked, "Mr. Greene asked somebody about what stuff we like? Who'd he ask?"

Sofia looked up to the ceiling as she thought for a second. "A babysitter or something? Chelsi, I think."

Piper nodded as a sudden lump came to her throat. "I miss Chelsi," she said quietly. "She was the best sitter ever."

Mr. Greene came into the kitchen followed by a white-haired version of a disgruntled Mary Poppins. Standing barely five feet tall and thin as a rail, Aunt Beryl did not resemble one bit of those smiling family photographs Piper remembered, except for her wire-rimmed glasses. The woman was dressed in a tailored dark gray pantsuit, and she wore her not-a-hair-out-of-place coiffure extremely short. Her face was made up flawlessly, and her lipsticked mouth was toying with a grimace. She wasn't frowning, exactly, but she wasn't smiling either. Wide, deep-set eyes analyzed the new humans in her kitchen as if trying to solve a difficult and smelly riddle.

After a few moments of awkward silence, Aunt Beryl nodded abruptly at Piper and said, "You look like your mother." Then she narrowed her eyes and spoke to Phoenix, frowning like she'd just tasted something rotten. "And you, young man, are the spitting image of your father."

Aunt Beryl noticed the dogs sitting in a quiet circle at Phoenix's feet, and her momentarily confused expression changed into a commanding stare as she pushed through a speech that sounded rehearsed. "Let's all agree to make the best of this unpleasant situation. I'm very sorry for the loss of your mother, but having two small strangers invade my home isn't going to be a cakewalk for me either." She clasped her hands together, her eyes lingering on Phoenix's new canine buddies as she continued. "Due to the fact that there are only ten weeks remaining in the Hancock County school year, I have notified the principal that in light of your recent trauma, the two of you will not be enrolling in public school this term."

No!

Piper's stomach dropped to her knees, and she had to work hard to choke down the bite of banana she had been chewing. She loved learning and tests and teachers and everything that most of her classmates hated about school, and she was looking forward with all her heart to getting back into a classroom full of books. And the thought of how Phoenix would do without the careful routine of a specialized school brought an even bigger lump to her throat. His daily routine would be up to her.

Piper stared at her cocoa, wishing she had a book in her hand to drown out Aunt Beryl's noise, or to throw at her perfectly combed head.

Aunt Beryl plowed on. "In the fall, I will consider what is best for Phoenix and his special situation, and I will decide what boarding schools will be the most appropriate choice for each of you." Piper wanted to interrupt, to explain that Phoenix needed his sister with him at school to protect him from bullies and untrained teachers and ignorant parents. But Piper wasn't yet brave enough to argue with this stranger.

Phoenix began to rock back and forth.

Aunt Beryl observed the boy's rocking with detached uncertainty as she marched through her lecture. "The only internet here is through a dial-up modem I use strictly for work. There is no Wi-Fi in the house, so don't bother asking. The public library in town has internet if you should need access for some reason, and Mr. Greene is available to drive you there on occasion. It should go without saying that running in the house will not be tolerated, and the dogs are not permitted to have any scraps from the table. The front parlor is off limits, as well as my study, my bedroom, my bathroom, and the library."

The library is off limits?

This cannot get any worse.

Don't cry.

"I'll be having the library remodeled in the coming weeks, and as I don't have a single children's book on the shelves, that room is strictly forbidden. Quite a few of the books are worth a king's ransom and are not to be handled by anyone but Mr. Greene and myself."

Aunt Beryl's voice suddenly became edged with frustration as she slapped her thigh and commanded, "Heel!" All three dogs jumped up from underneath the breakfast bar, coming to Aunt

Beryl's right foot and sitting primly in a row beside her, oldest to youngest.

Aunt Beryl nodded at the dogs with a grim and satisfied smile and then continued. "The estate sits on sixty-three acres of grounds and gardens that you are welcome to play in and explore, but I won't allow toys to be left out on the lawn under any circumstances."

Does she think we're babies? I'm thirteen; I don't have toys.

Don't roll your eyes.

"I understand that maintaining a strict routine is the best approach for a boy like Phoenix, so it works well that I have breakfast at seven every morning, taken here in the breakfast room. Lunch is at noon, dinner is at six, and both of those meals will be taken in the dining room. This schedule is not altered on weekends, and I expect you to arrive at the table free of dirt and with shirts tucked in. Mr. Greene has provided Sofia with all of your dietary restrictions, but she does not run a drive-through, so you'll be expected to eat what is provided and when, without exception. There is to be no eating anywhere but the kitchen, the breakfast room, and the dining room. Bedtime is at nine, and I expect the house to be quiet from then on. Do you have any questions?"

Aunt Beryl's pep talk had sucked the air out of the room, so Piper just shook her head. "No, ma'am," she responded. She chose not to expel the rude words jostling in her brain as Phoenix continued to rock back and forth, clutching half-eaten peanut butter sandwiches in both hands.

Because she knew that her mother would have expected her to, Piper added a rehearsed speech of her own. "Thank you for taking us in, Aunt Beryl. Even though Phoenix may not be able to show it, he appreciates you letting us come live here." She swallowed hard and added, "And so do I."

I believe that last bit may have been forced, Dear Reader.

Surprise brought a flush to Aunt Beryl's cheeks. She nodded and said, "I'll remind you that I didn't have much choice in the matter, but you're welcome. Come," she commanded. She threw one last confused glance at Phoenix before pivoting to exit the kitchen with Lincoln and Teddy at her feet. Quincy lingered, looking at Phoenix with a barely audible whine. "Quincy!" Aunt Beryl snapped from the hallway. Quincy reluctantly turned to obey his master, but his glum expression was proof to Piper that dogs could pout.

Mr. Greene shook his head with a smile. "Beats all I've ever seen," he said. "That dog hasn't cared a whit for anyone but your aunt for ten years, and now Mr. Phoenix here is the Dog Whisperer."

Phoenix made the finger sign for toilet, standing and shuffling from left foot to right foot. Piper pointed it out to Mr. Greene and Sofia. "See this thing he's doing with his hand?" She mimicked the sign, sticking her thumb between her first two fingers and twisting her hand from side to side. "Mom taught Phoenix some sign language, and that's how he tells us he needs to find the bathroom. He can do all the toilet stuff by himself, but he doesn't know where the bathroom is."

"Of course," said Mr. Greene. "The closest one is near the front door. There's a bathroom on the right as you come in, so make yourselves at home."

Piper grabbed her brother's hand, grateful for its soft familiarity in the middle of all this sharp newness.

I will never think of this place as home.

5

A Desperate Prayer

I was thirsty and you gave me something to drink.
—Matthew 25:35

Are you familiar with an interlude, Dear Reader? It's a respite, a hiatus, an interim, a pause-and-look-someplace-new part of the story.

That's what this chapter is: an interlude.

You might have assumed from earlier pages that the children's father no longer walked this earth, but you would be mistaken. So we leave the children getting used to their new house in Maine and go elsewhere. *Very* elsewhere.

It's hot here in this chapter, oppressively hot, a living heat that sucks all your energy away and makes even your eyelids sweat. If you have any hot cocoa left over from the earlier chapters, perhaps you should exchange it now for an ice-cold glass of lemonade and a little cardboard fan. Harsh, blistering dust may spill out from the next few pages. My apologies if a few grains of desert sand find their way into your socks.

Gordon Guthrie opened his eyes and looked around the dimly lit room. To say he opened his eyes is inaccurate. He opened the left eye, the one he could still see out of. The right eye didn't open any longer, no matter how much he wanted it to. He tried to sit up in bed, but the dizziness and pain in his head and behind his closed eye forced him back against the mattress, which was little more than a burlap sack stuffed with straw that smelled like a farm animal.

Fever raged through his limbs as he shivered, dressed in a thin, foul-smelling hospital gown that was pockmarked with stains he didn't want to think about. He pulled a threadbare cotton sheet up to his chin with his uninjured left arm and wished for the hundredth time for a simple glass of water. Gordon's right wrist was shackled with a short chain to the rusty metal railing of the bed, and his right arm hung limp, useless from the shoulder down.

A single bare light bulb was suspended from a frayed wire in the center of the room, a bulb that cast tired light over the gray cinder block walls and the concrete, sand-strewn floor. Besides the filthy gurney underneath him and a single stool on wheels, the room was empty. A solitary window, located up high near the top of one wall, allowed him an eight-inch-square view of a cloudless blue-white sky.

Gordon tried to remember what he was dreaming just before he awoke, but only tattered pieces of the dream came back to him now. He was splashing and running with Phoenix at the ocean while Piper and Naomi bobbed up and down out on the waves in a fat yellow raft. The sun shone on his wife's golden hair, and from this angle his daughter's flaxen curls shimmered in the light like alabaster china.

Each time the waves stretched up to meet his feet, Phoenix would squeal and laugh and run away from the approaching watery fingers in a tireless game of chase.

Lying alone in the concrete room, Gordon smiled, his chest aching as memories of his family both saddened and strengthened him.

I will see them again.

I WILL see them again, no matter what I have to do to get out of here.

He had lost count of how many days he had been in this place. The group of hooded men who had taken him captive outside his hotel more than two years ago had refused to answer his questions, simply screaming at him in a language he didn't know as they hurled him without pity into a military truck and drove into the desert. The men had treated him cruelly, as desperate men in times of war sometimes do, and he had been beaten so badly a month ago that his captors had brought him here to recover.

He didn't know why he was here, or why he was even being kept alive. Gordon didn't speak their language, having relied on an interpreter hired by the construction company to help him oversee the job site. He didn't understand why his captors didn't just do away with him outright. Perhaps they thought he could be ransomed for a tidy sum. Maybe they thought he was a spy or a high-ranking American soldier pretending to be someone else, but none of these things were true. He was an everyday construction worker, sent under contract by the American government to rebuild ruined hospitals and schools in a country torn apart by war.

Perhaps he resembled someone the hooded commandos had been seeking because they insisted on calling him "General," the only English word they knew. Each time he had said, "My name is Gordon Guthrie. I'm a builder. You've made a mistake," their cruelty only increased.

Gordon lifted his uninjured hand and felt around the wound on the shattered right side of his face, wondering how many stitches had been needed to close the gash. He counted nineteen stitches near his temple, plus six short strips of medical adhesive half buried in his swollen cheek.

A dark-eyed nurse had been tending Gordon since he was first brought from his underground cell into the concrete hospital above ground. Carrying a tray, the nurse shuffled into the room in bare feet as the bangles on her feet jingled softly. She was clad head to toe in a dust-caked gray robe with only her eyes visible. Bitter disappointment rose in Gordon's throat when he saw that the tray held no food or water.

The nurse opened a small vial and pulled out a shiny black blob that looked like a wiggling eyebrow. Gordon knew that leeches were still used by traditional healers to remove excess blood and swelling, and he was glad that the slimy critter's bite was painless. It still gave him the willies though. He tried not to think about a tiny Dracula sucking on his face.

Gordon winced in fresh pain as the woman roughly applied a foul-smelling ointment to the stitches. As she worked, he forced a smile through gritted teeth and asked, "So how bad is it, doc?"

The nurse's expression went from surprise to fear to resentment in a millisecond. Her eyes flashed with anger as she whispered, "It took all I know to keep you from dying, and if you die, they kill me." Her command of English was excellent, though it clearly wasn't her native tongue.

There wasn't a trace of sympathy in her voice. "You'll never see out of the right eye again; I'm sure of that," she said. "Don't expect an operation on the arm or the shoulder either. It would help, but they won't waste an operation on you. I'm just supposed to keep you alive, and that you are, for now."

Gordon watched the nurse put the lid back on the jar of ointment and wipe her hands on a cloth. The leech had its fill and surrendered, falling off of Gordon's eye onto his shoulder. The nurse scooped up the bloated creature and put it back into the vial.

The putrid ointment began to work, and some of the sharp pain was already subsiding. He let out a breath he'd been holding and looked into the nurse's eyes as he whispered, "My name is Gordon." Suddenly exhausted, he managed to add, "Thank you."

The nurse's eyes grew wide with shock and confusion, and Gordon caught the unmistakable glint of tears that sprang up in the corners of her eyes. She turned on her heel and fled the room with the tray, staring at her dusty feet as Gordon wondered what he had said to her to make her act that way.

Trying to get comfortable, Gordon halfway rolled over onto his uninjured side. Just as he had done almost every day of his life, he prayed, his thoughts focused and desperate as he whispered into the silence.

"Give me strength, God! I don't know why I'm stuck in this place, but I could really use some help in here.

"Give peace to Naomi and Piper and Phoenix, and somehow tell them I'm okay.

"Show me a way out of here.

"I'm so thirsty! You know I can't live without water, God, so You gotta help me out!"

Gordon's thoughts returned to the dream he'd had that night. Though he could only remember a fraction of the dream, his heart began to ache with longing as he pictured his family at the edge of the surf.

What's that you ask, Dear Reader? How can father and daughter have had similar dreams about the sea and a yellow life raft?

Perhaps you think this must all be a story, a fabrication, or merely a whimsical tale. You may argue logically that books cannot speak, dreams cannot be shared by two, and prayers cannot be answered.

I beg to differ.

The door swung open again, and the nurse padded into the room as she stared at her feet. Without a word she held out a cup of water to Gordon. He didn't care that the water was cloudy and lukewarm. It was water, and he drank it. He was too dehydrated to cry, but his voice was full of emotion as he handed her the empty cup and whispered, "Thank you."

The nurse nodded her head and shuffled to the door. That's when Gordon realized that the jingling noise wasn't made by bells or bangles on her feet. The nurse's feet were shackled together.

She was a prisoner too.

Gordon fell asleep praying for freedom, for his family, and for the nameless nurse who had given him a drink of water.

6

The Naming

The library is a trove of storied treasure
just waiting to be unearthed.
*–*Temperance Galligher

Let's get back to the children, shall we? Perhaps we should tiptoe through this chapter, Dear Reader. Sneaky sock-feet and zipped lips are a must.

Piper showed Phoenix where the bathroom was and as she waited for him to finish, she took the liberty of showing herself around. She stood in the foyer with the wide stairs to her left curving up and behind her. She poked her head into the parlor that Aunt Beryl had just included in her no-entry list. Judging by the parlor's décor, Piper wouldn't have been at all surprised to see Queen Victoria taking high tea at one of the room's glossy round tables. The lavish furniture didn't look like it would be comfortable in the slightest, and the gaudy flowered wallpaper went out of fashion decades ago. Thick velvet draperies in a dreary shade of green obscured the light from the lone window, in front of which was a gleaming black grand piano that was closed up and lonely for want of being played.

I will call you "Poison Ivy Parlor" because nothing in this room should be touched.

Assuming that Phoenix should be finished by now, Piper stepped back from the Poison Ivy Parlor doorway and headed toward the front entrance to find the bathroom open and empty. She didn't want Aunt Beryl to think she had misplaced Phoenix on their first day here, so she whispered, "Phoenix?"

He couldn't have gone very far in those few minutes, and it wasn't like him to just wander off. She opened the front door and heard a pleasant *Bing—Bong—Bing* warning chime from the security system somewhere, so she closed the front door, knowing her brother wasn't outside. Phoenix would have had to pass his sister to go upstairs, so he wasn't up there. She wandered through the foyer archway and into the Halls of Moria. She took a left, glad that her sneakers were silent as she tiptoed on the marble floors. At the opposite end from the fireplace, she went through an open entrance into a cavernous two-story formal dining room.

Paintings of country landscapes and formal British hunting scenes decorated the walls, and each painting stretched taller than Mr. Greene standing on tiptoe. Bright sunlight poured into the dining room. Opposite windows faced east and west, and one colossal row of windows took up almost the entire exterior wall of the house. The grand but lonesome occupants of the room included a mahogany china cabinet and matching buffet, a gleaming dining table with curved legs, and eighteen empty chairs. The table was so enormous that Piper stared at it for a while, trying to calculate how someone managed to get it through the doors and into the room. She finally gave up, figuring that the house must have simply been built around it.

You could feed two whole softball teams in here!

"Phoenix?" she repeated, louder this time.

The echo of her own voice in the dining room startled her.

"The Echo Chamber." Definitely calling this room the Echo Chamber.

She went back the way she had come and crossed to the other end of the Halls of Moria. She hadn't realized that there was an entrance to Aunt Beryl's library on the other side of the tall-enough-to-stand-in fireplace. Piper couldn't help but roll her eyes as she remembered what Aunt Beryl had said about the library.

No children's books? Phoenix and I love every sort of book; doesn't matter what kind it is. But of course she wouldn't know that. She doesn't know anything about us.

As she came through the doorway into the library, Piper was startled to find Phoenix already in the room. He was staring motionless into the very center of an expansive bookshelf on the long wall between the windows.

Dear Reader, he was staring straight at me.

Piper's surprise at finding Phoenix in the library dissolved into wonder as her gaze went around the room, drinking in the view like a starving man with a fork at an all-you-can-eat buffet.

Thick carpeting under Piper's feet swallowed the sound of her footsteps in a satisfying hush, and she came to stand beside the stone bust replica of some female ancestor staring off into space. Three pairs of large, comfy-looking armchairs begged for someone to plop down, switch on the waiting lamps, and read for the next twelve hours straight—perhaps someone much like you, Dear Reader.

From floor to ceiling on every wall, gleaming wooden shelves housed a collection of books whose beauty, number, and variety took the girl's breath away. There wasn't a single unoccupied space on the built-in shelves anywhere. It was a collection of which I was most honored to be a part.

Piper had to decide which was more interesting: whatever it was that Phoenix was staring at—because he never stared at *anything*—or the hundreds of books on dozens of bookshelves that begged her to lose herself within their promising covers.

She went to stand beside Phoenix, curious to see what was holding his rapt attention. For the last several years, Piper could remember only a handful of times when Phoenix had looked at anything for longer than a few seconds, except for when he was reading a book or eating a peanut butter sandwich. Piper stood next to her brother in the library they weren't permitted to enter, a few feet back from a shelf filled with valuable books they weren't supposed to touch.

Where is that weird blue light coming from?

Phoenix reached out and grabbed hold of Piper's hand with a strong, insistent grip as I spoke her name.

Piper.

She waited.

I spoke her name again.

She listened, turning her head and cocking an ear upward as her eyes narrowed, concentrating Beyond.

Above the silence, above the steady tick-tock of a stately grandfather clock in the corner, and above the rhythmic breathing of Phoenix, Piper heard it: the faintest of muted whispers. Curling from the bookshelf like an eddy of smoke around her ears, my salutation became a sigh without words that steadily increased in volume the longer she stood there. The murmurs drifted toward her from my unassuming origin—a fat, tattered book sitting on the shelf at eye level, dead center.

Welcome, Dearest Piper. I am honored to know you.

My brown leather binding was much shabbier than most of the other books in the room, and Piper squinted at the spine, unable to make out the faded title.

"Phoenix, we aren't supposed to be in here, buddy," Piper whispered. "It's . . ." She started to say something like "forbidden," or "off limits," or "not allowed," but she realized that the word-filled room needed a deserving name. Lifeless adjectives wouldn't do, and the perfect word jumped out of her memory from an old World War II movie she'd seen with her dad. "It's Verboten!" she hissed.

That's what this room will be: the "Verboten Library."

"There you are!" boomed a deep voice from the doorway. Piper jumped nearly a foot as Mr. Greene strode into the room with a bemused smile. "How about you let me show you to your rooms? All your things have already been unpacked."

"Sure," Piper answered, relieved that Mr. Greene hadn't scolded them for entering the Verboten Library. "Sorry. I just found him in here, but he usually doesn't wander off," she explained. "Phoenix, let's go upstairs and see where you'll be sleeping now." He let his sister lead him away from the bookshelf, but his gaze remained fixed on me with a focused curiosity and a longing on his face that Piper had never seen before.

I must add, Dear Reader, that I have never encountered such curiosity before or since.

As the children left the Verboten Library, Piper leaned close and whispered into her brother's ear.

"I heard it too."

It wasn't the last time the children would hear me speak. It wasn't the last time they would break the rules either.

7

Tales of a Thin Place

*The two words with power enough to set
a universe in motion are, "WHAT . . . IF."*
—Nita Orsini

The children followed Mr. Greene through the Poison Ivy
Parlor into the foyer and up the grand curving staircase to
the second floor. At the top of the stairs, an open balcony on
the right faced out over the vacant Halls of Moria, and the trio
walked down a hallway to where a second narrow staircase was
tucked away.

"Where do these stairs go?" Piper asked, peering down over
the handrail.

"That's called a service passage, and the stairs go down into
the kitchen," Mr. Greene explained. "And here we are at your
room, Phoenix," he said.

Phoenix walked into the room and turned around a few
times, looking and not looking at the same time. The enormous
bedroom was plain, with nothing colorful or artistic on the
walls. But it smelled fresh and clean and was equipped with a
sturdy oak twin bed and a matching dresser, mirror, and nightstand. The pastel blue bed linens were decorated with an assortment of cartoon dinosaurs, and the single window was dressed
in matching paneled curtains.

Piper strolled to the desk and pulled open the drawer. A pack of colored construction paper and extra-fat, toddler-sized crayons were inside next to a pair of blunt tipped safety scissors.

"Nice," Piper said, working hard to keep from rolling her eyes.

"And Piper, your room is right next door," said Mr. Greene. "Let's go have a look."

As they made their way from the room, Mr. Greene pointed left down the hall. "Washer and dryer are over there, should you need to make use of them when Sofia and I aren't available. There's a guest room just beyond. Your bedroom, and the bathroom you and Phoenix will share, is back this way toward your aunt's side of the house. Here we are," he said, opening the next door on the right.

Piper mustered up a smile as she entered her new room, taking stock of the pink ruffled bedspread and lacey curtains that any six-year-old girl would have loved. Besides the linens, the furnishings were identical to her brother's, down to the toddler-sized crayons, safety scissors, and bare walls. But two sizable windows looked out on the lawn and the tree-lined driveway, giving the room an airy feel. My spine began to tingle as Piper began mentally filling up the room with bookcases that went to the top of the ten-foot ceilings.

"I know it isn't home sweet home just yet," said Mr. Greene, "but give it time. Sofia and I will be happy to help you make it more to your liking. All of the things from your house in Atlanta will be delivered in the next few weeks, and if you want to rearrange the furniture or move anything around, I can help you with that."

"Bookshelves," Piper said with a nod. "I will need at least one whole wall of bookshelves. Make that two."

"An avid reader, are we?" Mr. Greene asked with lifted brows and a smile. "There's a great reading spot behind the garden, and you can see straight out to the ocean from there. I can show you and Phoenix if you like, once you're settled in."

"Oh, Phoenix *loves* the ocean," Piper said as she moved one of the curtains away from the window. Just then she saw a fluffy orange puffball dart across the lawn and disappear around the corner of the house. "Aunt Beryl has a cat?!" Piper asked with a grin.

Mr. Greene said, "Your aunt tolerates the presence of two outdoor cats. They're permitted to make residence here under the inflated assumption that they keep mice out of the garden."

Piper said, "Mom was allergic, but my dad and I always wanted a cat."

"Shall we see if we can track them down?" asked Mr. Greene.

Excited by the prospect, Piper leapt out the door intending to run down the master staircase at full speed. Then she remembered Aunt Beryl's icy warning about running in the house. Exercising enormous self-control, Piper fast-walked down the stairs and donned her jacket as she impatiently waited for Phoenix and Mr. Greene to catch up.

A few minutes later the three of them were outside with their coats on, walking down the front steps into a gray and chilly April afternoon. "Here, kitty, kitty," Piper called a few times, snapping her fingers. "What are their names?" she asked.

Mr. Greene said, "The orange one you saw earlier is Mouser, and we just call his brother Kitty. He's black."

"*Kitty?* Oh, that won't do at all," Piper said. "Phoenix and I will find him an appropriate name once we get to know him. Mouser is a good name though."

"Kitty is a loner, so getting to know him may be a challenge," Mr. Greene explained.

"Still, we'll have to find him a better name. You said he's black, right? We could call him Mr. Mistoffelees after a black cat in the *Old Possum's Book of Practical Cats*. It's one of my favorites."

Mr. Greene laughed. "That's quite a mouthful!"

Have you read about Magical Mr. Mistoffelees, Dear Reader? How about his friends Grizabella and Old Deuteronomy? I do enjoy the ink-and-paper variety of cats, but not so much the teeth-and-claws living sort. Such prickly creatures do not always mingle well with paper.

The U-shaped driveway was lined with colossal evergreens, quite different from the scrawny scrub pines that were so familiar to the children. A portion of the driveway in front of the house was paved in gray cobblestone to match the old-fashioned Tudor design. Piper, Phoenix, and Mr. Greene walked around the left side of the house, the lawn so perfectly manicured that Piper feared her shoes would leave unwelcomed tracks in the sod. Around the back there was a miniature Tudor-style cottage Piper hadn't noticed before. It was connected to the main house by a covered walkway. "Who lives there?" Piper asked.

"You've discovered my humble abode!" said Mr. Greene. "My apartment is through this front entrance, and Sofia has a separate apartment around the back. Ah!" Mr. Greene was interrupted by a mewing sound. "Here's just the man we've come to find. Good afternoon, Mouser. Have you earned your keep today?"

A fat orange tabby with eyes the color of marigolds wandered across the grass and began purring and rubbing Piper's shoes with his face. She picked him up and nuzzled his fur, her heart softening and thawing as a drop of affection trickled out. "Oh, my goodness, you're so sweet!" she whispered. Mouser leapt without warning from her arms and began winding around

Phoenix's legs, purring and nuzzling the boy's shoes as he stood still.

The back door flew open and Lincoln, Teddy, and Quincy bounded across the lawn toward them. Sofia poked her head out the door and waved as she said, "They said they wanna join you!" All three dogs assumed the same position as before as they sat nearly motionless at Phoenix's feet and gave him their undivided attention.

"They don't bother the cats?" Piper asked. Instead of giving chase, Mouser had calmly stepped aside to avoid the canine stampede.

"When Lincoln was a puppy, he got it in his head to chase Mouser one night. I'd swear the cats had a secret strategy meeting, because the next morning both Mouser and Kitty ganged up and ambushed Lincoln when he came around the corner of the house. He learned his lesson," said Mr. Greene. He leaned over with a wry smile and tapped a long white scar running down the center of Lincoln's nose.

Then Mr. Greene pointed to a low stone wall that ran the entire length of the house, a wall that formed an enormous rectangle to the rear. "After a visit to England fifteen years ago, your aunt had the formal garden put in, and she spends her free time caring for the roses. Sofia just started prepping the ground for an herb and vegetable garden near the kitchen. Apparently she's got quite the green thumb and loves to grow things!"

"You said before that you can see the ocean, but I can't see it from here. Where is it?" Piper asked.

"Of course," he replied. "Right this way."

The formal garden was filled with dozens of symmetrical boxwoods and identically trimmed evergreen topiaries alternating with rosebushes. Stone pavers, laid out in neat squares, created a crisscross path through the thick grass that was just beginning to turn from winter brown to spring green. Piper said, "Back in our Atlanta neighborhood, we had a tiny old house with three pine trees and two azalea bushes."

Mr. Greene said, "I'm sure it seems overwhelming right now, being your first day here. But I think you and Phoenix will come to love it. There is—"

"Where's Phoenix?" Piper interrupted, looking back toward the house. For the second time that day, Piper feared Aunt Beryl's wrath for losing track of him. "The new surroundings have him all out of whack, but I promise, he's not a wanderer," Piper said. "At least, he didn't used to be back in Atlanta."

Mr. Greene turned his back to the house and pointed toward a line of trees at the far edge of the lawn. "He's over there, and the dogs are with him," he said.

"Oh, okay, I just couldn't see him for a second," Piper said. "He won't run off and climb a hundred-foot tree or try to scale a water tower or anything. But he likes being outside and listening to the wind, even if it's cold."

Mr. Greene and Piper walked along in silence for a while, and she was glad that the butler didn't feel the need to fill the frosty air with words. She felt guilty for taking up all of his time when he could be back at the house doing butler-type things for Aunt Beryl.

The pair came to the end of the formal garden wall and turned right. Phoenix was still with the dogs at the edge of the forest, and Piper followed Mr. Greene through the grass along the garden wall. He stopped at the far corner underneath the leafless, spreading branches of a mammoth sugar maple tree. Piper thought she'd never seen a tree this big in her life.

Mr. Greene pointed to the base of the tree and said, "If you want to see the ocean, you'll have to climb."

"Climb the tree?" Piper repeated.

With a nod Mr. Greene said, "You're wearing jeans and sneakers, so why not? It's quite a view from up there, and it makes a fine reading nook. There aren't any leaves on the tree yet, so the view of the ocean will be even better." He gave a mock frown and said, "Don't tell me you're too old to climb trees!"

"Wait, how do you know what the view is like from up there?" Piper asked, eyeing Mr. Greene's long and lanky legs with doubt. "Have *you* climbed it?"

Mr. Greene raised one eyebrow and pretended to be insulted. "Do you doubt my ability to climb a tree, young lady?" He laughed at Piper's guilty smile, and his expression became thoughtful as he gazed up and beyond the branches. "I climb it often, actually. For lack of a better explanation, this particular tree seems to be a thin place."

Piper's brow furrowed. "Thin place?" she echoed, squinting into the sky through the leafless limbs. "You mean, like there's less air up there or something?"

"Not exactly. The notion of a thin place goes back to the Celtic peoples of Ireland and Scotland," he explained, "and probably even long before them. Certain places in the landscape were considered sacred, and something about those lands set them apart. The people believed that heaven and earth are normally about three feet apart, but when you're in a thin place, heaven is much closer. They said it was easier to sense the presence of God when you're in a thin place."

Piper shrugged and kicked the trunk of the tree with her toe. "I don't think I believe in all That Stuff anymore," she said, pretending she didn't have a sudden ache deep in her gut.

Mr. Greene looked beyond Piper as he sucked in a sudden deep breath. "Oh, my," he said quietly.

Piper turned around and was greeted by a mud-caked mass of fur. Wet clumps of cold black sludge fell in big globs onto her pant legs and shoes. Lincoln was barely recognizable underneath a coating of swampy muck.

"Gross!" Piper yelled, waffling back and forth between laughter and disgust. "Lincoln, what have you gotten into?" She was glad the muddy canine had showed up just then so she didn't have to explain to Mr. Greene why she didn't believe in That Stuff anymore.

Of course, Dear Reader, she *did* believe in That Stuff. She simply assumed That Stuff didn't believe in *her*, or that It had taken her parents away and abandoned her in Maine with her little brother. She just couldn't put all that into words.

We'll hear more about that later.

Approaching from the tree line, Phoenix meandered through the grass, looking up at the sky with something close to contentment on his face. Quincy walked alongside just inches from the boy's feet. The old dog's gray coat was also adorned with a few extra pounds of thick mud. Teddy brought up the rear with his own collection of slime dripping from every inch of his fur, except for his glorious red tail and muzzle. There wasn't so much as a speck of dirt on Phoenix, and Mr. Greene looked on with a bewildered smile.

"Is there a pond or something over there?" Piper asked, curious about where such an enormous volume of mud came from.

Mr. Greene nodded. "There's a fresh-water spring that comes out of the ground just down that way, and I guess the spring snow melts have come early. Care to lend me a hand with clean-up, Piper?"

"I've always wanted to give a dog a bath!" Piper said.

As the muddy canines followed their humans across the grounds, Piper said, "Aunt Beryl is going to freak out, isn't she?"

Mr. Greene shook his head. "Part of my job is to ensure that no freak-outs take place on my watch."

Sofia opened the back door with a grimace as the crew approached from the garden, and she was already decked out in elbow-length rubber gloves and a giant pair of green galoshes. Wielding a scrub brush like a sword, she grabbed Lincoln's collar and declared, "Do not pass go, and do not collect two hundred dollars!"

8

Longing for Lost Things

They were just words. But they were
the words she needed to say and couldn't,
so she found them in a book instead.
−Enitan Clark

*B*eep! Beep! Beep!
  A warning sound chimed outside the window an hour
after lunch, and Piper jumped from her bed where she had been
reading to look outside. When she pulled back the curtains, she
saw a large white delivery truck in the driveway. "Our stuff is
here!" she shouted. Not caring that she was breaking the no-run-
ning-in-the-house rule, she hoofed it next door to her brother's
room and found him asleep on his bed.

"Wake up! Our stuff is here, Phoenix!" Piper shouted as she
bounced on his bed.

My books are here!

Phoenix and Piper had been at Aunt Beryl's house—their new
home—for ten days. Besides the muddy dog incident early on,
nothing diary-worthy had happened. Without the internet or
cell service those first few days, Piper thought she would go mad
with boredom. Mr. Greene hadn't been able to take the children
to the library in town yet, but playing with the dogs, watching
Mouser scamper after birds outside, and keeping a watch over

Phoenix had kept Piper busy enough. The new daily routine wasn't anything like what Phoenix was used to back home, and many times Piper relied on the soothing presence of the dogs to help calm her brother's frustrated rocking. When the energetic company of three adoring pets didn't work, Piper resorted to showing him photos of their parents on her cell phone, and that seemed to make him feel better—sometimes.

With no way to keep in touch with the outside world, Piper figured her friends back in Atlanta thought she had fallen off the planet. She had finally stopped checking her phone for service and used it instead for listening to music and playing tedious games in which she had no interest. At night, when she missed her parents the most, she would scroll through photos of her mom and dad as she cried herself to sleep.

There were only a few things Piper had found herself really missing from her old house. Her collection of books was at the top of the list, of course. The books in Piper's old bedroom had been selected and arranged by her since she could read at the age of three. During the confusing years before her brother's autism had been diagnosed, those books never failed to lift Piper's spirits, or at least take her mind off things she didn't understand.

The perfect outfit to wear while reading those books would be a thick red Atlanta Falcons hoodie that her mom had given her for her birthday last October, and she looked forward to finding it. This cold Maine spring weather definitely called for more hoodies and warm clothes, considering that they had woken to a dusting of snow the day before yesterday.

The clock radio Piper had kept on her nightstand back home was at least thirty years old and had belonged to Gordon when he was young. It still worked just fine, and the greenish glow-in-the-dark flip numbers were funny to look at. Piper was anxious to have it back and try to at least find a radio station.

Her laptop was next on the list of things she was impatient to have back in her possession. Naomi had saved every one of their family photos onto a thumb drive, even scanning all the old ones that were printed into photographs before the world went digital. A couple of months before Naomi died, Piper had copied the entire library onto her laptop. There were several thousand photos in all, and I could feel Piper's heartache when she tried to picture both of her parents' faces and found it hard to reconstruct them all the way. Piper had also saved some of her favorite movies on the laptop, and she looked forward to sitting up in bed at night watching movies with Phoenix after lights-out.

Piper came downstairs and found Mr. Greene and Aunt Beryl standing at the open front door as a duo of deliverymen made their way inside. Each man wielded a hand truck with a stack of five identical boxes, and each box had a single word written in bold black marker on the side. BOOKS. Piper shivered as the cold air rushed into the entryway.

"Basement," Aunt Beryl barked at the man with the hand truck. "Through the foyer, left down the hall, there's a door on the right in the kitchen."

"What?" Piper shouted. "Wait! Those are mine!"

Aunt Beryl ignored Piper's outburst as the two men avoided eye contact with the girl and carefully maneuvered past with their hand trucks. Piper felt the red blotchiness of anger rising in her neck and face as she watched the men disappear down the hall.

"Books don't go in the basement!" Piper said as her bottom lip began to tremble.

Aunt Beryl crossed her arms and stared hard at Piper as she said, "You are in my house, and you will abide by my rules, like it or not. They're going to the basement." Her command left Piper no room to argue or ask any more about the fate of her beloved books.

Soon a third deliveryman appeared at the front door with another box-laden hand truck. These five boxes were marked PIPER'S THINGS. Aunt Beryl frowned at the deliveryman and said, "I won't have that hand truck scuffing up the stairs."

Mr. Greene reached out to take the top box from the hand truck. Finding it quite light, he handed it to Piper and picked up the next two boxes easily. "Lead the way, Piper," he said brightly. The deliveryman grabbed the last two boxes, and Piper reluctantly led the group up the curving staircase. She fought back tears, not giving in to her urge to stomp the whole way up.

Piper put the box on her bed and slumped down next to it. Mr. Greene put his two boxes on the floor as the deliveryman did the same. "Would you like Sofia to come help you unpack?" Mr. Greene asked gently.

"Those are my books!" Piper said loudly, not caring if Aunt Beryl could hear. "She has no right."

Mr. Greene came to the bed and knelt in front of Piper. "As soon as I can get it arranged, we'll get a proper set of bookshelves installed in your room. Old books or new books—either way, we'll fill those shelves soon. I promise," he said.

One enormous tear refused to stay put, and Piper smashed it down hard with her palm. "Thanks," she whispered. "I didn't even know you *had* a basement."

Mr. Greene patted Piper's shoulder and nodded. "It's your basement too, Piper. It's a good basement, nice and dry. Your books will be safe down there for a few weeks. I'll send Sofia up to help you unpack the rest of your things."

Piper couldn't do a thing for her imprisoned books at the moment, so she did her best to ignore her anger and turned to the box on the bed. The heavy-duty packing tape wouldn't budge, so she jammed a pen between the cardboard flaps and wrestled the box open.

Sort of like a weird Christmas morning.

This first box was filled with everything that had been on Piper's nightstand the day her mother died. Looking at the contents made her smile, even though her heart was hurting and squeezing and heavy. The messy stack of books that had been piled on the nightstand wasn't there.

But Gordon's old electric flip-dial clock radio was inside, wrapped in plastic bubble wrap. Piper unwrapped it, plugged it in next to her bed, and set the time, planning to scan for radio stations later. Next she unwrapped her favorite swivel-arm reading lamp and placed it next to the clock on her nightstand exactly the way she had it in her old room.

"About time your stuff got delivered," said Sofia as she came into the room still wearing her apron. She had tied a bright orange kerchief around her head in a futile effort to tame the wiry curls protruding every which way, and it looked as though a bird could happily nest on the crown of her head. "Here's some scissors if you need help getting these boxes open," she said as she produced a pair from her front pocket. "Would you take a look at that old clock! I had one just like it when I was a kid."

"It's my dad's," said Piper.

Over the past two years, she'd grown used to her father's absence, so she was unprepared for the sudden rush of sadness that came over her when speaking about him. Mom was her connection to Dad, and now Mom Was Not, so it felt like Dad Was Less. And she didn't know what to do about that.

Piper swallowed hard, cleared her throat, and said, "I'm hoping I can get some sort of radio station up here."

"Do you want help unpacking?" Sofia asked. "It's totally up to you, and if you'd rather do it alone, I won't get my feelings hurt. Scout's honor."

"Sure," Piper answered. The only things left in the first box were pencils, a clip-on battery-powered booklight, five bookmarks in search of a page, a loved-hard stuffed bunny with floppy ears, and a small folded piece of paper. Piper realized in an instant that it was the note Phoenix had left for her before dinner that stormy night back in March. She stuffed the little note into her jeans pocket to decipher later.

Piper arranged the stuffed bunny in a sitting-up position on her pillow, not caring how childish it might look. Then she put the other items on the nightstand.

Sofia opened the second box with the scissors and found it packed full of neatly folded clothing from Piper's old closet. "My Falcons hoodie!" Piper yelled, grabbing it from the top of the stack. She buried her face in the thick fleece as Sofia retrieved a handful of empty hangers from the closet. The hoodie still smelled like the old house, with the lingering aroma of Naomi's favorite fabric softener.

A profound ache began to swell in Piper's chest, and she blinked back a few tears as she breathed in the fading scent of a different life. "I have missed this thing!" she said, tugging it on even though she wasn't cold.

When she pulled the hoodie over her head, the memories trailing along with the scent of that sweatshirt overwhelmed her with images of her mother, and all she could do was sit down on the bed and give in to the tears. Sofia sat down next to Piper and wrapped her arm tenderly around the girl's heaving shoulders.

Sofia let Piper have a good cry. Then she pulled a cloth hanky from her apron as she whispered, "I miss my mama, too."

Piper wiped her nose and looked up at Sofia. "You do?" she managed.

She nodded, wiping away a tear of her own. "She died a few years ago after a long fight with cancer. Even though we knew it was coming, I was *such* a mess after she died. I cried all the time at first, and my heart was squeezing so much it was like I could hardly breathe sometimes. But when I needed to cry, I did, no matter if I was in the car or the store or the post office, or wherever. Didn't care, didn't hold it in, 'cause I just couldn't. And then one morning I woke up, and I could breathe a little easier, and I realized my heart wasn't squeezing so much. Then another day, and another day, and then a month, and another month, and then before I realized it, a whole year had gone by, sun still coming up, me still breathing, and life still going on." She patted Piper's hand and said, "Sweetie, you take all the time you need. One day the missing won't hurt your heart so much."

Piper nodded, hoping that what Sofia said would be true as she took a deep breath and trudged back over to the box to continue unpacking. She kept the hanky in her pocket in case she needed it again.

They put all of Piper's coats and hoodies into the closet and moved on to the next box, which contained everything Piper had kept on top of the dresser. Dozens of photos she'd kept wedged into her old mirror frame were packaged neatly in a zip-top plastic bag, and Piper put every one of them in as close to its old spot as she could remember on her new mirror over the dresser. Phoenix when he was a baby; Gordon looking for shells at the beach; Piper's eleventh birthday party; Naomi winning an Ugly Christmas Sweater contest at church; Piper and Gabriella in the sixth-grade play; Phoenix on the first day of school last year. By the time Piper was finished, the photos went down both sides of the mirror and across the bottom. She stood back to admire her handiwork for a second before Sofia gave her several more things from the box. She laid out a white lace doily, a little jewelry box, some tea-light candles, and a strand of miniature white Christmas lights. Piper draped the light strand across the top of the mirror and plugged it in.

Sofia's face lit up with approval. "Amazing what a little love and Christmas lights will do to a room," she said. "It's *much* happier in here now."

Piper finished unpacking her clothes boxes, and the final box contained all of the artwork that had been on Piper's old bedroom walls. Piper looked around the improved surroundings, wondering if Aunt Beryl would allow her to make holes in the walls.

"Oh!" said Sofia, reaching into her apron pocket and bringing out several packages of adhesive picture hangers. "Mr. Greene gave me these in case you wanted to hang anything on the walls."

In a few minutes the two of them installed a large metallic peace symbol over Piper's headboard, a black and white framed shot of the Eiffel Tower on the left wall, and three small sepia prints on the right wall. The sepia prints, showing a series of abandoned buildings in downtown Atlanta, were ones Piper had taken herself.

Piper stood in the center of the bedroom and looked around with approval as Sofia started cleaning up strands of packing tape and shredded bubble wrap. "*Now* this is starting to feel like my bedroom," Piper said.

"I'm heading to check on your brother," Sofia said. "Will he need help unpacking?"

"Oh, shoot. Yes!" Piper answered, feeling guilty about forgetting him for so long.

Piper had an idea. She grabbed the photos of Gordon and Naomi from the mirror and took them with her into her brother's room.

Phoenix was sitting cross-legged on his bed drawing on some construction paper. The stack of PHOENIX'S THINGS boxes waiting by the door hadn't been touched.

"Let's get you moved all the way in, buddy," Piper said, trying to picture as many details of his old bedroom as she could. Piper did her best to put his things in a similar place here, and she placed the photos of their parents on his nightstand.

In the middle of the ups and downs of remembering and smelling old clothes and opening boxes, Piper completely forgot about Phoenix's old cipher note that she had shoved into the pocket of her jeans.

9

A Bit of Thievery

*I wonder what tales you might hear if your
grandfather's bookshelves could speak.*
–Lance Murdock

Piper glanced at the glow-in-the-dark dials on her clock radio. 12:06.

Aunt Beryl should be asleep now.

She found her bootie slippers in the dark with her toes and pushed her feet in. Her Atlanta Falcons hoodie was draped across the footboard where she'd left it as she made her plans earlier in the day. She slipped the hoodie on over her pajamas.

The destination?

The basement.

Her books were calling her, and they had been calling her since being banished to the deep, dark dungeon basement forty-two hours ago.

Of course, Dear Reader, they weren't calling to her the same way I did. But those books were her treasures and her comfort, and she missed them deeply.

All three dogs slept in Aunt Beryl's bedroom at night, crated separately so they didn't combine forces and cause mischief. Aunt Beryl also slept with her bedroom doors closed, so Piper was sure the dogs wouldn't hear her if she could be quiet enough.

She fished the little clip-on booklight from its hiding spot inside her pillowcase where it was stashed for possible power-outage emergencies and for reading past bedtime. She clipped it to the front pocket of her hoodie, then bent it down to illuminate her path. The entire house was still unfamiliar to her in the dark, and she didn't want to stub a toe on any unexpected corners or furniture.

Aunt Beryl did not tolerate squeaky doors, floors, or hinges, so Piper was grateful for a silent flight of service stairs. Piper had previously assumed that particular door in the kitchen was a closet. She had never opened it until she sneaked a peek yesterday afternoon, confirming that it was indeed the entrance to the basement. Piper opened the door, took one step down, and closed it behind her. She stashed the booklight in the pocket of her hoodie and flipped on the light switch.

When the lights came on, her concerns about a dank and dusty cellar with book-gnawing critters or concealed bogeymen were erased. The stairwell walls and bright lights looked like the storage rooms at her mother's office building: bare, clean, and completely free of anything remotely haunted. The spacious basement ran underneath half the house, and at the bottom of the stairs Piper stepped onto a plain tile floor. It didn't even smell like a basement. It smelled like Office Depot, and not a single creepy shadow or cobweb was visible.

A dozen pieces of furniture sat against the far back wall, each covered with furniture padding. She recognized some legs and edges as belonging to the old furniture from her house in Atlanta, and Piper's heart leapt when she saw four empty wooden book-cases against the wall to her right. She made a mental note to remind Mr. Greene of his bookshelf promise first thing in the morning.

Ten boxes filled with Piper's books stood in two forlorn stacks in the middle of the room. She wasn't looking for any books in particular. She'd already decided to open just one box, grab the top five books, and make her escape quickly to lessen her chances of getting busted. She still had the scissors from Sofia, so she cut carefully through the packing tape of the box closest to her. She reached in, grabbed the top five books without looking at them, and then grabbed one more really fat one because she just couldn't resist.

Enough! Don't push your luck!

Before she caved in to her desire to cart every single book upstairs to her room where they belonged, she folded the flaps back in on themselves and patted the box lovingly. "I'll be back for all of you soon, I promise!" she whispered.

As she came to the top of the basement stairs and turned off the light switch, a muffled noise reached her ears.

Don't be alarmed, Dear Reader. It was my voice she heard.

Piper froze, listening hard as she awkwardly clutched six books to her chest. The basement door was still closed, and she could have sworn she saw a hint of pale blue light coming in underneath the doorway from the kitchen. She didn't dare turn on the booklight for fear that someone passing by could see it, and she held her breath as she pressed her ear against the basement door.

It was hard to hear anything over her own heartbeat pounding in her ears, but after a few long seconds, she heard the noise again.

Whispers.

I've heard those whispers before.

Piper's fear gave way to an overwhelming curiosity, and she eased open the basement door handle and poked her head out. The appliances, pots, and pans were all sleeping as they should be, and there was enough moonlight shining in through the windows for her to see that the kitchen and breakfast room were unoccupied. Piper silently closed the basement door behind her and made her way down the service passage hall, right through the archway into the foyer, and then left past the master staircase into the darkened Poison Ivy Parlor. My whispers grew louder in Piper's ears with each step.

The luminous whiteness of Phoenix's pajama top was clearly visible through the Poison Ivy Parlor doorway into the Verboten Library. Phoenix was standing in the same spot as he was the first time Piper had caught him in there, his gaze riveted to the very center of the longest bookshelf a few feet in front of him. Piper tiptoed into the library and placed her stack of books on the floor before moving to stand by her brother.

Still staring at the books, Phoenix reached out to take his sister's hand. My spine began to tingle and resonate with unread words, and Light and Truth and Story began to flow from within and seep out of my pages.

Piper blinked, and her mouth dropped open as she watched a pale blue light begin to pulse and grow, radiating out from the bookshelf into the air and flooding the room with Otherness.

I didn't mean to frighten her, Dear Reader. But each time a New Story begins to bubble and rise and make itself known, my pages simply can't hold it in.

Phoenix turned his head to look at Piper.

He *really* looked at her, directly into her eyes for several long seconds.

The last time he looked at Piper like that, he had been five years old.

Tonight his eyes had lost some of the amber color, a bright sparkling emerald taking over and visible in the whirl of bluish light. Piper felt like Phoenix could see all the way through to the inside of her brain.

He finally turned his head back toward the center shelf. His body was motionless, all traces of his usual rocking movements on pause as he stared and listened to me.

"I hear it," Piper whispered. "I don't know what it's saying, though. Do you?"

Piper and Phoenix stood there in the whispering, swirling light for several minutes, breathing in the scent of thousands of pages in hundreds of leather and linen bindings around us all.

I wonder, Dear Reader, if you've ever heard about the chemistry of old books and the names of certain compounds that give them the sweet-dusty-almond-glue-and-ink-and-flower smell that so many Readers love. That unmistakable scent, ancient and new, filled the atmosphere of the library as Promise became a tangible thing.

Piper stepped closer to me as she fished the booklight from the front pocket of her hoodie with a trembling hand. The leather binding on my hardback spine was so worn that Piper had to twist the light back and forth to see what was once visible there, the remnant of a title embossed in faded gold letters.

"*Novus Fabula*," she whispered, wrinkling her nose. "Is that Latin? What does that even mean?"

Phoenix let go of Piper's hand, stepped forward, and pulled me from the off-limits shelf.

The room became dark again.

The whispering stopped.

"Phoenix," Piper whispered sharply. "We're not supposed to even *be* in here! If Aunt Beryl sees that a book is missing, there are exactly two people she'll blame for stealing it!"

I feared that Phoenix was going to put his prize back on the shelf. Instead, he reached over to where Piper's basement-rescued books were waiting on the floor and took the top one from the stack. Then he put that book in place of the one he had poached, the fat replacement filling the open space on the shelf perfectly. He pressed a crumpled note into his sister's hand and moseyed upstairs with his plunder.

But Piper could not bring herself to leave just yet. Out of curiosity, she turned the booklight in the direction of the shelf to see which of her books Phoenix had selected for the stand-in. When she read the title, she stifled a laugh. Her brother had shelved Piper's one and only copy of *Harry Potter and the Order of the Phoenix.*

10

Cryptic Ciphers

King Solomon says it be the glory of God to conceal
a matter, but the honor of kings to seek it out.
Crown or naught, 'tis you be such a king, my boy.
—Edwardus Padrick

P iper still stood in the Verboten Library, staring at the darkened bookshelf for several long moments with her mouth
open.

Did that really just happen?

She pinched herself in the arm and winced.

Ow! Not sleepwalking.

The sleepiness and confusion were simply too much, so Piper
shook her head, grabbed her books from the floor, and tiptoed
upstairs to her room. Using her booklight, she deciphered the
note Phoenix had just given her.

6-26-5, 47-22-6, 36-12-6, 99-5-6, 99-14-9, 24-22-3

Decoding the numbers took barely a minute.

"new story wanting to be read"

Then she made an entry in her diary before finally falling
asleep.

Dear Dad, I really, really, really wish you were here so I could tell you about what just happened with me and Phoenix in Aunt Beryl's library. Creepy but not creepy, like cool and magical. Sounds crazy, but I promise I'm not making it up!

Was Uncle Lonnie like some kind of magician or something? Because there's this book....

If you ever come home, I'll try to explain it then, but I think this book might be enchanted or something. I don't know. But I know Phoenix heard it too, so I'm not crazy.

Not to worry, Dear Reader. Piper and I will meet when the time is right.

The next morning Piper woke to the aroma of sausage. She dressed and brought her book-filled backpack downstairs and set it on the floor next to her as she sat at the breakfast bar. She was looking forward to spending the entire day reading her rescued books.

Aunt Beryl had breakfasted earlier and was already in her study. To Piper, Aunt Beryl's absence was an enormous relief. Meals with Aunt Beryl were stiff and quiet and awkward because she didn't believe in talking at the table.

The pungent scent of spicy sausage made Piper's mouth water, and she watched Sofia carefully crack an egg into a small cast iron skillet. Producing a perfect sunny-side-up egg, Sofia turned the skillet upside down over a plate filled with crispy fried potatoes, onions, chorizo, and green peppers. She set the plate in front of Piper with a large glass of milk and said, "Chow time!"

Piper's stomach rumbled with anticipation. The runny egg yolk infused the whole dish with a rich yellow sauce when she poked it with her fork, and she cleaned the plate in a matter of minutes. "You have to show me how to make this one day!" Piper said. "Will you teach me?"

Sofia grinned wide and said, "Absolutely! Any time you're ready, just say the word."

The chorizo was spicy enough to make Piper's nose run, and the cold milk cooled it down nicely. "I'm not sure how Phoenix will feel about this breakfast," she said. "He's not big on spicy food."

Phoenix came into the kitchen and took a seat at the breakfast bar. Piper smiled as she realized he was carrying the photo of Gordon she'd left on his nightstand the day before.

Phoenix put his nose directly over his breakfast plate and took several deep whiffs. He tried one bite of a fried potato, then pushed the plate toward Piper and put his head down on the table.

Sofia patted his shoulder and magically produced a plate of peanut butter and jelly sandwiches she'd tucked away in the fridge. "Good job, Phoenix, trying a taste of some new stuff!" she said. "We'll keep trying, and maybe we can find you some new favorites." Sofia smiled as Phoenix started in on the sandwiches, but she left the breakfast plate nearby just in case.

Piper watched Phoenix enjoy his breakfast. Then her thoughts jumped from Phoenix to unpacking his room, to unpacking her room, to unpacking her father's clock radio. Her stomach dropped to the ground when she remembered that while Sofia was helping her unpack yesterday, Piper had shoved that old cipher note into her jeans pocket and forgotten about it.

Piper swallowed hard. "Today is laundry day, isn't it?" she asked.

Sofia nodded. "Yep. Last of your stuff went in the wash just a few minutes—"

Piper jumped from the stool and flew up the service stairs two-by-two. (It was hard, Dear Reader, to always remember the No Running in the House rule.) She wrenched open the washing machine lid and saw her jeans on the top, almost fully immersed in the sudsy water. She pulled the jeans from the water and found the note in the back pocket, relieved nearly to tears that it was just a little damp. She closed the washer and took the note downstairs to decode. "Saved it!" she said triumphantly as she smoothed it out on the breakfast bar.

Sofia laughed. "Acting like you were chased by a hornet!" She squinted at Piper's note and said, "What's that? Some sort of numbers game, or a math thingy?"

Piper nodded. "It's kind of like a numbers game, I guess. It's from Phoenix, and this one was from our old house back in Atlanta. I unpacked it yesterday but forgot about it in my pocket."

Sofia said, "Close one!" She shook her head and said, "I gotta remember to check pockets from now on."

Piper sat back down on the stool and fished *The Giver* out of her backpack, decoding the cipher as she finished her milk.

8-8-3, 41-8-3, 156-26-8, 171-6-2, 100-17-1

She looked at the words she had deciphered.

"Mother will go into light"

She double checked the pages, lines, and word numbers to make sure she had read them correctly.

"Mother will go into light"

Of course, she did. She died, and she went into the Light, and that's what everybody says happens when—

Wait.

Piper stared at the note in her hand, and her vision went blurry as tears of wonder and disbelief welled up in her eyes.

Phoenix had written this note some time *before* dinner that awful day back in March, many weeks and miles and a lifetime ago. Naomi had called from work about nine to tell Phoenix and Piper good night before the thunderstorms had even started, but the note was already in Piper's bedroom by then. She clearly remembered moving the still-unread cipher note aside to look at the time on her clock radio when Naomi called home, like she always did, to say goodnight prayers with both of them over the phone.

Phoenix knew.

Before it had happened, Phoenix knew.

11

Verboten, Invaded

The books didn't want to be dusted;
they wanted to be devoured.
−Tajana Baird

Phoenix?" Piper whispered, searching his face for something that would clue her in as to how he could have known ahead of time.

Piper couldn't see that I was hiding under her little brother's shirt. Phoenix took a long chug of milk and stuffed Gordon's photo into his pocket. Then he reached under his shirt and pulled me out onto the counter. I found myself next to Piper's elbow, and her words escaped her.

After being filched from the off-limits library, I had stayed up all night with young Phoenix, Dear Reader. He knew my secrets now, cover to cover. And I knew his.

Sofia had been busy at the sink this whole time, so she hadn't seen Piper's astonished expression, or me, or the faint aura of pale blue light hovering in the air above the breakfast bar. Piper leaned over, grabbed me, and covered me with her crossed arms, intending to return me to my spot in the Verboten Library later that night when everyone was asleep.

You may wonder, Dear Reader, why Piper didn't take me to her room to read straightaway. With all of the ups and downs she'd faced since her arrival in Maine, her sturdy little soul was weary, and confused, and afraid. After all, it is a bit odd to hear a book whisper and see it glow. I didn't mind waiting. Piper knew I was special, and she would also know when the time was right.

Phoenix wiped the milk from his upper lip and turned his whole body to look at Piper, straight into her eyes, for the second time in as many days. He leaned forward and slipped yet another of his scribbled notes into her palm.

Sofia turned from the sink with her hands on her hips and looked at Phoenix as she asked, "Did you get enough to eat, kiddo?"

Phoenix pulled the untouched breakfast plate toward him and took another long whiff. He picked up another fried potato and popped it into his mouth, then pushed the plate toward Sofia as he chewed and swallowed. Sofia cleared the dishes, oblivious that Phoenix was doing things Piper hadn't seen him do in several years.

Still trying to make sense of everything that was happening, Piper completely forgot about the backpack on the floor as she stood and tucked me nonchalantly under her arm. "I think we'll go find a place to read for a while," she said, hoping her voice didn't betray the fact that she was aiding a thief and concealing stolen property. "You coming, Phoenix?" she asked, walking to the doorway of the kitchen and nodding her head forcefully in the direction of the hall. Phoenix followed.

The children walked in silence down the hall, and I began to speak to Piper again. I knew deep in my spine that Piper needed to hear the story I had for her.

Piper was sure the whispers were echoing loudly enough for everyone in the house to hear, and she was afraid someone could see the pale blue light shimmering in the air. She stopped in the middle of the hallway and pressed my front cover against her ear as she tried to tune in to the Story that floated from the binding. It seemed that Piper could almost make out words, but they were just beyond her grasp, like chasing a piece of a dream that is out of memory's reach.

The front doorbell chimed.

Piper heard the front door open, followed by the pleasant *Bing—Bong—Bing* alarm. Mr. Greene's most professional butler-voice said, "May I help you?"

"Ashley Carrington of Carrington Designs," said a harsh, nasally voice. "I have an appointment with Ms. Bouchard." The children heard high heels clicking on the hardwood floors of the entryway, and Piper grabbed her brother's hand instinctively.

"Good morning, Miss Carrington." Aunt Beryl's voice responded from somewhere above their heads. Piper could tell that Aunt Beryl was coming down the main staircase.

If she catches me with this book in my hand and sees that it's one of hers, we're dead meat!

Dragging Phoenix along, Piper ducked left under the second archway and tiptoed into the Halls of Moria. Assuming Aunt Beryl would take Ashley Carrington of Carrington Designs upstairs to the study, Piper pulled Phoenix along behind her through the Great Hall, past the giant fireplace, and around the corner into the Verboten Library. The marble floors and high walls of Moria, combined with the openness of the main staircase and the archways, caused voices to echo and travel and bounce around, leaving Piper bewildered. She heard voices and had no clue where they were coming from.

The nasally voice sounded again, growing louder and closer. "You received the design packet I sent out last week?"

Piper stood next to Phoenix in the middle of the Verboten Library and remembered back to the day they had arrived. Aunt Beryl had said something about remodeling.

They're coming in here!

Piper suddenly adored the hideous floor-length draperies that Aunt Beryl employed at each of the four library windows. The children slipped behind one of the thick fleur-de-lis curtains seconds before Aunt Beryl and Ashley Carrington of Carrington Designs came into the library from the Poison Ivy Parlor.

"Yes, I did receive it," Aunt Beryl said. "Everything appears in order, and I am ready to move forward with the project."

Dear Reader, you should know, that although I'd spoken and called her name for decades, Beryl Bouchard had not yet heard me. This broke my heart, but I would continue to try, with the knowledge that I did have a story to tell her. She would hear me when she was ready.

"Wonderful," crowed Ashley Carrington of Carrington Designs. "I see you already have a fully stocked library, but you mentioned on the phone that you were interested in the *Books by the Inch* program. The books we'll provide for this project are simply stunning, and we can supplement with volumes we'll order from the Beguiling Bookshelf Company. Are you still leaning toward that option?"

"Yes," Aunt Beryl replied curtly. The two women walked through the library, unwittingly coming nearer to the children's hideout. "These old books are all different shapes and colors and sizes, and they are terribly messy, with no symmetry whatsoever. You said the books will all match?"

"Oh, yes, ma'am," gushed Ashley Carrington of Carrington Designs. "*Books by the Inch* are identically matched for size and binding color to your specifications, and we have a wide variety of spine and title color options for you to choose. I'm sure you'll be pleased with how symmetrical and tidy the whole library will look when the installation is complete."

Symmetrical? Tidy?! Libraries aren't supposed to be symmetrical and tidy! That's like saying every flower in the world has to be the same shape and color! It's like telling all the people on earth that they have to be the same weight and skin color and height and wear the same clothes as everyone else, and telling all those same people they can't get dirty or take detours or visit new cities or get lost. No two people are alike, and no two books are alike either!

I must say that I agree with Piper wholeheartedly, Dear Reader.

The two adult voices were moving away from the curtained hiding place. Phoenix stood motionless, staring straight ahead at the back of the curtain panel as if nothing was amiss.

The sharp voice of Ashley Carrington of Carrington Designs continued. "The new books will all be bound in the finest leather, with each title embossed on the spine in gold or silver; your choice. Do you have any preference as to subject matter? Classics? Biographies?"

"It makes no difference," Aunt Beryl replied. "They will only serve as decoration."

Who has space for this many books and doesn't plan to read them?

Piper found herself liking the newcomer less and less.

"Wonderful," cooed Ashley Carrington of Carrington Designs. "Our proposal includes leaving all these gorgeous built-in shelves as they are. May I ask what your plans are for the existing collection? I see a number of high-quality antiques and first editions on the shelves. Perhaps you're planning an estate sale, or an auction for the rare book collector?"

The greed dripping from the irritating voice of Ashley Carrington of Carrington Designs made Piper want to kick the woman in the shin.

"Oh, I don't care what happens to them after they leave here," Aunt Beryl said. "Too many bad memories wrapped up in this room. They're being auctioned off to the highest bidder in a week."

"NO!"

Piper jumped out from behind the curtain, not caring that she was eavesdropping in the Verboten Library, and not caring that she was holding one of Aunt Beryl's off-limits, untidy, non-symmetrical books, and not caring that she was interrupting a meeting between adults.

"Aunt Beryl, please," Piper begged, tears springing to her eyes and desperation taking hold of her voice. "Please don't sell them! I promise I'll take good care of every single book, and I will put them all into boxes and store them in the basement for when I grow up and have a library of my own. You'll never have to see them again, but please don't let somebody else take them!"

Ashley Carrington of Carrington Designs had cried out and jumped a foot off the floor in her high heels when Piper leapt from behind the curtain, but Aunt Beryl was unflappable. She was coifed and prim as always, with flawless red lipstick and a tailored houndstooth jacket. She narrowed her eyes at Piper and opened her mouth to say something.

But she was interrupted as Mr. Greene came into the room. "Miss Guthrie and I will take full responsibility for the old books, madam," he said diplomatically as he put his hand on Piper's shoulder. "I assure you they will be stored out of sight, and there is no need to wait for Miss Carrington's team to begin the removal process."

At that moment, Piper loved Mr. Greene more than anyone else in the world.

I'm terribly fond of him myself, Dear Reader.

Aunt Beryl gave an abrupt nod. "Fine. It makes no difference to me. You may have the books, Piper, if you and Mr. Greene can have the library emptied within the week. Any books remaining after next Saturday will be sold. No exceptions."

Ashley Carrington of Carrington Designs scowled openly. She looked back and forth between Mr. Greene and Piper like a cat eyeing a plump canary that had flown just out of reach.

"Very good," said Mr. Greene. "Piper and I will get to work." Mr. Greene looked at Piper expectantly. She resisted the urge to hug him and cry and thank him all at the same time, and she simply nodded.

As Aunt Beryl and Ashley Carrington of Carrington Designs headed out of the Verboten Library, Aunt Beryl stopped and turned to look at the thick draperies by the far window. Phoenix was still hidden, still immobile, invisible to them all. Piper was glad he couldn't see the icy glare being directed at him.

"There had best not be any peanut butter on my draperies, young man," Aunt Beryl warned before she marched out.

Ashley Carrington of Carrington Designs glared at Piper, and the designer's face was scrunched up as if she had just swallowed a bite of something rotten. Piper stared back at the designer and stuck out her tongue as far as it would go. Ashley Carrington of Carrington Designs lifted her chin and followed Aunt Beryl from the room.

12

Unexpected Help

Be astonished! Be astounded! For a work
is being done in your days that you
would not believe if you were told.
—Habakkuk 1:5 NRSV

G ordon tilted his head forward as life and warmth seeped
into his throat and spread into his empty belly. Groggy and
weak from fever, he obediently sipped the steaming cup of liq-
uid the nurse pressed to his lips. He tasted some unfamiliar and
stringent herbs with maybe a hint of beef broth, but he didn't
care what was in it. It was warm, and he was starving.

The dark-eyed nurse was still barefoot and wearing the same
dirty gray robes that covered everything but her eyes. "Quickly.
All," she whispered, glancing behind her toward the closed door.

Gordon took the cup from her with his uninjured hand and
downed the contents as tears of gratitude sprang to his eyes.

The nurse reached into the folds of her clothing and pulled
a tiny yellowed envelope from a concealed pocket. She dropped
five little white pills onto the dingy mattress beside him. "Take
these," she demanded. "One you take now, second one tomorrow,
third the next day, understand? All five. Do not miss any."

He was almost too surprised to form words. "How—?" he
began.

"Medicine," she whispered, looking back at the door. "Help with infection."

Satisfied with her answer, Gordon popped the first pill into his mouth and swallowed it dry, wishing he had a gallon more of the savory broth. It was the first meal he had eaten in many weeks, and he wondered what sort of healing herbs she had added.

The grimy burlap mattress on which Gordon lay had a hole in one of the corners. He pushed the four remaining pills into the hole with his free hand and tried to smooth the mattress out as best he could.

The nurse nodded in approval as Gordon lay back down, and she continued her leech treatment the same as before. She removed the creature from its little vial on the tray at the foot of the bed and applied it to the still-swollen tissue beneath Gordon's eye. Then she applied the rank-smelling ointment to the wound, and there was no mistaking the change in the nurse's touch. She was gentle this time. She glanced at him and saw a tear trickling down his face, and she pulled her hand away from the wound. "This hurts you?" she asked.

He smiled as another tear escaped. "Not really," he responded. "Just grateful, that's all, and confused as to why you're helping me like this. It's dangerous."

She shrugged her shoulders and looked at the floor. "You said thank you," she said. "No person has said those words to me in the three years I've been kept here, and I've bandaged up more bloody and broken men than I can count. I'm already in danger, so a little more will not matter."

As the nurse finished the treatment and put the leech away, Gordon didn't hide the emotion in his voice as he whispered, "Thank you, again." Though only her eyes were visible, Gordon saw the woman's expression soften in response.

The nurse took the empty cup and tucked it somewhere inside the layered folds of her clothing seconds before the door burst open and one of the captors stormed into the room. He began screaming at the nurse in his language as his hands gestured wildly in the air.

Gordon let his head droop to the side, half-closing his good eye and mustering up a series of convincing moans. The soldier stopped yelling and lowered his arms, the raging anger in his expression becoming less certain. He came close, his face just inches from Gordon's nose, and Gordon pressed his lips together under pretense of pain, praying the man wouldn't be able to smell the broth and herbs on his breath. The soldier sniffed, and Gordon held back a smile when he remembered he hadn't been anywhere near a bar of soap, a shower, a stick of deodorant, or a proper toilet in more than two years. Recoiling at the stench, the soldier wrinkled up his nose and spat on the floor in disgust.

The nurse bowed toward the soldier and said a few quiet words to him as he backed off. Grunting in frustration as he stalked from the room, the soldier slammed the door behind him and caused Gordon's insides to rattle.

Through his half-open good eye, Gordon saw the nurse's pinched shoulders relax as she let out the breath she'd been holding. She took the tray and left the room without looking back, her shackles clinking as she shuffled out.

Oh, Jesus, please protect that young woman! Heal this body so I can see Naomi and Piper and Phoenix again!

Thank You, God, for soup and for medicine and for hearing my prayers, and for Your faithfulness. I don't understand what's happening, but I know You are here with me, and that's enough.

The simple meal of broth was small, but it made him warm and full enough to fall into a deep, restful sleep.

13

Piper Meets Her Collection

Holding court between the stacks, I consult with kings.
I confer with wizards there,
who whisper wondrous things.
Sages wise, and foolish lords, with merit and without,
I stand them up, all spine to spine,
and watch them duke it out.
—Riordan Teague

Piper looked around the Verboten Library with a sinking feeling in her stomach. She lost count of the number of books that were quietly waiting to be relocated. She'd been given the deed to a gold mine without realizing she was the pack mule.

She rubbed her fingers over the binding of the book in her hands one more time. She acknowledged that she couldn't read and box up books at the same time, so her appointment with me would have to wait.

Mr. Greene said, "If you'll accompany me to the basement, Piper, we can bring some empty boxes upstairs and get started. Shall we?"

Piper nodded and glanced at Phoenix as he emerged from his hiding place behind the curtain. "You wanna come help?"

she asked, not sure if he would be of much help but hoping he would join in.

He responded by coming toward Piper and taking her hand. "I guess that's a yes," she said. "I just have to run this book upstairs to my bedroom, and I'll be right back." The book she was talking about, of course, was me. She placed me on her nightstand, next to *The Giver*, which made me feel special.

By the time Piper made it up to her room and then back down two floors to the basement, Mr. Greene and Phoenix had already begun carrying stacks of flattened cardboard boxes up the basement stairs. Piper smiled when she heard Mr. Greene talking to Phoenix as if he was just like every other boy in the world. "I went ahead and picked up all these empty boxes a few weeks ago when your aunt told me what her plans were for the library," Mr. Greene said. "I like to be prepared."

Piper picked up the remaining flattened boxes and two rolls of packing tape that were nearby and followed her brother back up the stairs and into the Verboten Library.

After all these years, Dear Reader, I knew precisely the marvelous company I had been keeping on these shelves. But Piper hadn't had a chance to examine any of my distinguished shelf-mates, and she was excited to see what her literary inheritance contained. "I promise not to start reading any of the books as we start packing them up," she said.

Mr. Greene laughed as he taped up the bottom of several boxes and readied them to receive a load of books. He said, "Piper, you can take these two empty boxes and start over near the parlor door. Phoenix, you start here between the windows, and I'll start over on the other side. As you fill one, tape it closed, and then stack it in the center of the room. Let me know if you need help lifting."

The first set of books Piper grabbed were all written by Charles Dickens, an author she had heard about and always planned on reading. I'm honored to have been in bookish company with the likes of *Oliver Twist* and *Great Expectations*.

Curious as to how old the books were, Piper took one of the Dickens books from the shelf and thumbed through the front pages. She almost dropped it when she saw the year of publication. "This says 1873!" she said, turning to Mr. Greene in shock.

"That's the Dickens illustrated edition," said Mr. Greene with an approving nod. "Such a fine collection. I believe there are thirty books all together. Devil of a time tracking down *A Tale of Two Cities*, but I finally found one and completed the set eight years ago."

Piper couldn't imagine how much money a set of books like this had cost. She began to handle them less like paper and more like antique china.

Mr. Greene said, "All these books belong to you now, Piper. Perhaps you'll consider opening a bookstore of your own one day. Ever thought about it?"

She nodded and kept working, filling and taping a box, and filling and taping another box. "I think I'd like to be a bookbinder, the person who gets to repair antique books," she replied. "Then I could travel all over the world and handle some of the oldest books ever made, with gloves on of course."

Mr. Greene nodded. "Of course!"

"There's a story I read once about a bookshop where the books were sold out of the back of a horse-drawn cart. Have you heard of that one?" Piper asked. She began to work up a sweat.

"Yes," said Mr. Greene. "It was called *Parnassus on Wheels*. My mother was a librarian at the Chicago Public Library downtown when I was growing up, and she loved that book. Oh, how she could read aloud! Every week she had story time in the children's wing, and I swear she could mesmerize the worst hoodlum in the city just by reading them a story. She helped start a bookmobile outreach too. Not as exciting as a horse-drawn cart, mind you. But the bookmobile did go all around Chicago, to every single neighborhood that had a kid, even if it was just one."

Phoenix sat on the library floor reading the first thing he'd pulled from the shelf, a thin blue book called *Poems* by Edgar Allan Poe. Piper just smiled and shook her head, happy to see her brother doing one of his favorite things.

Mr. Greene said, "Years ago, the need to settle your uncle's affairs after his death took me to the United Kingdom on a buying assignment. Books he'd contracted to purchase, the ones specified in his will, that sort of thing. The horse-drawn bookshop you mentioned reminds me of a town called Staffordshire. It has a floating bookstore on a barge where they sell books on the water."

Piper stopped and stared at Mr. Greene with a piece of tape dangling from her fingers. "Wait. My *uncle's* books?" she repeated. "These books were *his*? I thought these were Aunt Beryl's books."

Mr. Greene's eyebrows furrowed in confusion. "I thought you knew all about your Uncle Lonnie," he said, filling another box.

"I've heard a little about him from my dad, just enough to fill in a family tree for social studies class, but that's it. Did you know him?" Piper asked.

"Oh, no," said Mr. Greene. "He passed away four years after your aunt and uncle were married. Lonnie made his living buying and selling rare and collectible books, and his will included a long list of instructions about completing this library. That's one of the things your aunt had me do when I was first hired a few years after he died."

Mr. Greene sighed. "She wasn't always such a hard woman," he said. She loved the books as much as Lonnie did, and she was bent on fulfilling his last wishes. But over time, without someone close to share them with . . ." He trailed off and shrugged his shoulders. "She wasn't the same. The longer the books sat there, the more she wanted them to disappear."

He shook his head and said, "Anyway, we were talking about the shops I've been to. I went to a shop in Paris that was housed in an old train station. Wonderful place."

Piper stopped to wrestle with a piece of packing tape that was stuck to itself. "If I were to open my own shop," she said, "I would have part of the store outside, maybe like a courtyard with climbing flowers, and some of those big wooden carts with wheels so the books could be rolled outside each morning."

Mr. Greene's eyes twinkled as he said, "Perhaps every now and then, would someone happen upon a magic book in your shop?"

I sensed Piper's heart speed up a little as she thought about me sitting upstairs in her room. She was beginning to believe that things weren't always as they seemed.

"Movies and TV shows are the only places I know that have magic books sitting around," Piper said, hoping she sounded convincing.

"Oh, I wouldn't be too sure," said Mr. Greene with a sly smile. "I read a story about one bookshop where all the books could fly."

"Are you talking about *The Fantastic Flying Books of Mr. Morris Lessmore?*" Piper asked. "I read that book to some kids when I was babysitting last year, and they loved it. But one of the kids wanted to make his book fly like Mr. Lessmore's did, so the next day he decided to send a brand-new copy of *Green Eggs and Ham* out a third-story window into the swimming pool, and it didn't turn out so well for the book."

Mr. Greene laughed as Piper continued.

"There's a part in the book where it says, 'Everyone's story matters,' and my mom always said that sentence was like her life motto," Piper explained. "She even had that quote framed and stuck on her desk at work."

"I love it," Mr. Greene said. "What did your mom do for work?"

"Mom was an editor at a publishing company," Piper said. "Sometimes when she wasn't sure if a new manuscript was any good, she'd bring it home and let me read it before anybody else had ever seen it. Then she'd ask me all sorts of questions about it. I was like her test subject," she said with a proud grin.

"Now it's all making sense!" said Mr. Greene.

Filling yet another empty box with books and taping it closed, he said, "This room always reminds me of a movie called *The Time Machine*. In the very last scene, you discover that the time traveler has returned long enough to take three books from his library before setting off to an unknown time. They never tell you what year he went to, or which books he chose."

The next item she pulled from the bookshelf was a two-volume packaged set titled *Oxford Latin Dictionary*. Thumbing through the definitions took longer than she expected, since the stiff and stubborn pages had never yet met a Reader, a fact that made me terribly sad.

Piper looked up the word *fabula* first, and found it translated as "story." Then she looked up the word *novus* and laughed aloud when she put them together.

Novus Fabula.

New Story.

Phoenix said the new story wanted to be read, but I sure didn't know he could read Latin!

Sofia popped her frizz-ball head around the corner. "Okay, everybody has to stop packing books, wash your hands, and get in here for lunch, pronto!" she demanded. Phoenix was still buried in the poetry book he had begun when the project had started, so Piper went over and tapped his shoulder.

"Lunch time!" Piper said.

As the three of them abandoned the mess in the Verboten Library, Mr. Greene said, "Sometimes I've thought about what books I would take with me if I were crazy enough to jump into a time machine with a three-book limit. What about you?"

"There's too many to pick from!" Piper said. I sensed her thoughts return to me at that moment as she said, "I have all my old favorites, of course, and . . . well . . ." She pictured her brother plucking me off the library shelf a few nights earlier as she added, "Since Phoenix would be with me, he'd have to bring his favorites too."

I wonder if Mr. Greene can hear it.

By that evening, Piper was exhausted from the work in the library. But she had thoughts bubbling in her brain that she had to let out into her diary before bed.

Dear Dad,

I wish you could've been here today! Aunt Beryl has all these awesome books from Uncle Lonnie, and she was gonna chuck them, but they're mine now! There's a ton!

I guess I never thought about how she would miss Uncle Lonnie. I mean if it was me, I'd want all his books around me all the time, but she doesn't even want to look at them. I guess that's her way. Not how I'd be if I was her, but she's just DIFFERENT.

14

On Everywhen

Oh, you already know everything about everything?
How dreadfully dull.
—Cordelia Adams

W here'd you go yesterday?" Piper asked.
Mr. Greene was seated on the small porch of his cottage
engrossed in a book when Piper ambled out of the house with
Phoenix late on a Sunday afternoon.

"Rugby match," he replied. "I try to make it into town at least
twice a month on Saturdays to play with the league there."

Piper's mouth dropped open. "You play rugby?" she asked.
"Isn't that like football in the mud without a helmet?"

Mr. Greene laughed. "Exactly like that!" he said. "Started
playing as a teenager and can't find a reason to quit. Keeps me
from getting flabby and stale as I get older."

Piper nodded, finding it hard to picture Mr. Greene dressed
in rugby shorts and striped knee stocks, running from a team
of muddy men. Then she spied the book in his hand and asked,
"Whatcha reading?"

Mr. Greene cleared his throat and began to recite aloud.

"I stand alone in the vast and friendless dark.

Behind me: smiling faces, light, ease, the empty comforts
of yesterday.
Before me: a lonely sigh in the void of tomorrow.

Fear clutches at my throat as I totter and sway upon a
brink I cannot see.

Do I go back?
Do I step forward?

I see a scroll appear before me, a worthy parchment spread
out wide.
As a painter wields his brush,
creating vibrant strokes and vivid hues as he determines,
I, too, must fill these empty pages
with words all my own
in a language of my choosing.

With a flourish I snatch the quill from my previous world
and turn my back to yesterday
as the light behind illuminates the uncertainty ahead.

I let the Author take control.
Each drop of ink becomes a work in itself as I step forward,
making and being made;
forming and being formed;
writing and being written;
my Story."

As Mr. Greene recited these words, the ink on my pages
began to sing and tremble. There was something mesmerizing
about the way his voice wrapped around each phrase and coaxed

it to life. His deep, lilting tone didn't merely read the words. His voice embodied them, empowered them, and gave them a heartbeat.

Piper's eyes were closed as the poem washed over her. "Whoa," she whispered, opening her eyes. "That was awesome. Who wrote that?"

Mr. Greene said, "It was written in 1986 by a teenager named Beth-Anne Elison. She died in a tragic drowning accident just a few months after she wrote this."

His sobering comment made Piper love the poem even more. Though she still pretended not to believe in all That Stuff anymore, she said, "For some reason it reminds me of that thing you talked about before, about the big tree at the edge of the garden being a thin place. Remember telling me about that?"

Mr. Greene nodded as he gazed out at the lawn. "Oh, yes," he answered. "In fact, this book I'm reading is about that very thing." He held up the cover for Piper to read.

"*Life on the Edge of Everywhen*," she recited. Her brows furrowed at the unfamiliar term. "Everywhen?" she repeated. "What's that?"

"What does *everywhere* mean?" Mr. Greene asked with a patient smile.

"Well, duh," Piper responded. "All places at once."

"And how about *everyone*?" he continued.

"All people, like everybody," she answered. "And *everything* is, like, every single thing. All the things at once."

"Good. So, using that same logic, tell me what 'everywhen' would mean," he said, leaning forward with an expectant smile.

Piper spent a few moments with her thoughts, staring up at the sky before responding. "I guess it would mean all the time, sort of like always, but bigger. I don't know . . . it's hard to explain. Like no beginning and no end, maybe."

Mr. Greene touched his finger to his nose with a wide grin and said, "Ding! Good answer, young lady. It's all of time, every moment that has ever happened or ever will happen. We have such small brains that it's hard for us to think about things without time getting in the way, but time is a man-made invention. It helps my little head to realize that God isn't just every*where*, but He's also every*when*, before me, after me, writing this unending story that I'm a small part of. Gives me a little perspective, I suppose."

"So what's the edge of it then?" Piper asked.

"Excellent question, Miss Prodigy," Mr. Greene said. "This is how I look at it. We're so wrapped up in ourselves and our lives and our problems that we think *this* is all there is," he said, waving his hands in the air and gesturing to the sky and the cottage porch. "Most of us walk through life with an invisible wall around us, unaware of what exists outside our imagination. Sometimes, in certain places or during certain moments, that wall becomes thin, so thin that it's like a curtain, or a transparent veil. So as far as I see it, living on the edge of everywhen means you constantly press into that veil, listening, searching, and watching for it to be stretched so thin that it disappears."

Piper was silent for a few long moments. Then she swallowed hard and whispered, "So, what's on the other side?"

Mr. Greene leaned forward with a cryptic smile and a lifted brow as he said, "You tell me. I already have my answer, but you'll have to discover it yourself. Truth be told, I think the 'thin place' analogy could make us expect far too little of God."

"I don't know what you mean," Piper said.

"Well, since God created every place in the universe, He can make us aware of His presence in any place at any time He likes, instead of just being confined to church, or to some far-off heaven, or to those thin places. We should even *expect* Him to be here, right where we are. If we look for Him, we might see Him in places we don't imagine an all-powerful Creator would be."

At a loss for words, Piper cocked her head sideways and said, "Huh."

"I read something that said grown-ups don't see magic because they stop looking for it," Mr. Greene said as he gazed thoughtfully at the sky. "I never want to stop looking."

I can't tell you, Dear Reader, how thrilling it is when a gentle soul like Mr. Greene examines a mystery in search of Truth. It makes my spine tingle.

15

Night Walker

With trembling hands she held the unread letter to the light. Immortalized by pen and ink, the words of the dead raced forward from a bygone era to speak to her.
—Oscar Wesley

Piper opened her eyes and blinked, the night so thick it made no difference whether her eyes were open or closed.

Can you see well enough, Dear Reader? Darkness oozes out from the pages of this chapter. An extra flashlight is recommended to keep the grabbing shadows at bay.

Why am I awake?

Piper felt it again: a nudge against her elbow at the edge of the bed. She heard soft breathing and caught the familiar whiff of peanut butter.

"Phoenix?" she whispered. Her eyes began to adjust to the darkness, and her brother's silhouette came into focus beside her. Piper reached out and found his hand, and he began pulling her hard.

"Hang on!" she whispered, untangling the bed sheets and blankets from her legs without letting go of his hand. "What's wrong?" she asked. She stood and found her slippers with her toes, wiggling her feet into them as Phoenix continued to tug.

"I'm coming!" she whispered as she found her bathrobe and pulled it on. "I have a flashlight under my pillow; one sec!"

Phoenix let go. Piper tied the sash of her robe, reached into her pillowcase, and pulled out the booklight. "Okay. What is it?" she whispered. She clipped the light to the sash, switched it on, and pointed the beam toward the ground.

Phoenix grabbed his sister's hand again, and she let him lead her out of the bedroom, down the hallway, and past their shared bathroom toward Aunt Beryl's chambers. "We aren't allowed to go in there!" Piper whispered, but something told her to trust Phoenix anyway. He led her around the corner and into Aunt Beryl's private study.

In the shadows cast by the small booklight, Piper made out the shape of an imposing desk on the inner wall. On the opposite side of the room, a pair of matching Queen Anne chairs upholstered in some pale shade of glossy fabric took up space in front of the window that overlooked the back garden. Skirting the antique chair legs and a claw-foot round table, Phoenix pulled Piper all the way up to the window so that their noses were brushing the glass. He stared down at the darkened grounds below while gripping Piper's hand, agitation and frustration evident as he stamped back and forth. Piper switched off the booklight and waited for her vision to adjust as she stared outside into the darkness.

The late-April moon was half full, hidden at that moment behind a slow-moving cloud. Piper could just make out the dark silhouettes of budding tree branches trembling in the night breeze, and a dewy mist crept ghostly and thick around the base of the topiaries. It curled down from the garden and floated toward the far-off tree line.

Piper noticed a shimmery patch of something moving inside the garden wall nearest the house, and her breath caught in her throat as the clouds parted and a dim shaft of moonlight spilled out over the manicured grounds. At first Piper thought she was seeing Lincoln, but then she realized that retrievers don't normally walk on their hind legs and do not, for the most part, wear flowered nightgowns.

There's no such thing as ghosts.

Piper tried and failed to swallow her fear in a suddenly lumpy throat. Then it dawned on her that this phantom's ankle-length gown was printed with large pink roses in a pattern better suited for a sofa than a ghoul.

Aunt Beryl?!

"What is she doing out there?" Piper whispered.

The flowered apparition moved sluggishly among the evergreen topiaries. She stopped to bend over every few minutes and pull the foliage apart to peer into the woody depths of each shrub.

Phoenix yanked his sister's arm and pulled her out of the study, down the hallway, and toward the main stairs. It was all Piper could do to keep from tripping in her slippers. She switched the booklight back on to illuminate their path down the stairs, through the archways, and into the frigid Halls of Moria. The back door in the far left corner of the ballroom stood wide open to the night, and the children hurried outside.

"We should go get Mr. Greene!" Piper whispered. Phoenix let go of her hand and headed toward the topiaries.

Piper rushed to the cottage apartment and was relieved to find the front door unlocked. She went in without knocking and found her way to the single bedroom door.

Mr. Greene was clad in blue checkered pajamas, sleeping like a mannequin posed in a mattress commercial under a nearly crumple-free blanket. He lay flat on his back with his hands crossed serenely on his chest. Piper patted the butler's crossed arms. "Mr. Greene, wake up!"

Piper wondered if the American Butler School in New York taught its students the art of waking gracefully when being shaken from sleep by a frightened child. If Mr. Greene's reaction to her was any clue, the answer is yes.

"Good evening, Piper," Mr. Greene managed, sleep thick in his voice. If he was startled by Piper barging into his room, he hid it well. "Is everything all right?"

"It's Aunt Beryl," Piper whispered. "She's outside in her nightgown, and I don't think she's remembered to put on her shoes." Piper swallowed hard, surprised by a sudden concern for her aunt's well-being. "I think she's sleepwalking or something."

Mr. Greene's drowsy face became fully alert. He slipped on a pair of sneakers that were on the floor beside the bed and grabbed his glasses from the nightstand as he stood. Pulling a jacket from behind the bedroom door, he said, "I'm glad you woke me. This isn't the first time this has happened, and her doctor told me the best way to handle your aunt's episodes."

What episodes?

Piper followed Mr. Greene through the tiny cottage living room to the front door she had forgotten to close, shivering as she stopped in the doorway. "Do you need my flashlight?" she offered, holding the booklight up to Mr. Greene.

He smiled and shook his head as he bounded down the cottage porch steps. "No, thank you, Piper; the moon gives me plenty of light to see. I would be most appreciative if you could go around to the other apartment and wake Sofia for me. It's easier with two."

Mr. Greene stepped into the grass, and Piper jumped when she heard a sound out in the yard to her left. The soft beam of a flashlight bobbed on the ground, coming toward them from around the other side of the building. Sofia came into view and whispered, "I got up to go to the potty and I heard voices out here. Everything okay?"

Sofia's wayward hair was free from its workaday bun and even more unruly from a case of bed-head. Wiry strands of silver-tinged hair stood up in every direction like an electrified Medusa. She was typically clad in a no-nonsense apron and sensible shoes, but now she sported a bright purple set of polka-dot pajamas and fluffy bunny slippers.

"She's sleepwalking again," Mr. Greene said.

Sofia nodded. "Ah. I need better shoes; be right back."

Sofia ducked back into her apartment where she donned a bathrobe and exchanged her slippers for a pair of sneakers. She joined Mr. Greene and Piper a minute later, and Mr. Greene led the way to the garden.

Piper almost ran into the back of Mr. Greene as he came to a sudden halt in the grass.

"Would you look at that," Mr. Greene whispered.

Piper and Sofia looked up to see Phoenix leading Aunt Beryl toward the house. He was in front of her, walking backward, holding both of her hands and gently pulling her in the direction she needed to go.

Mr. Greene looked at Piper and gave the universal "shush" sign with his finger to his lips as they watched Phoenix lead Aunt Beryl into the house. Sofia and Mr. Greene followed in silence, and once everyone was inside Piper pulled the back door closed without a sound.

Aunt Beryl was transformed into a creature Piper barely recognized. The put-together, demanding, bossy woman Piper thought she knew had been replaced with an ancient and shuffling old woman with sagging eyes that were confused and half-open. Phoenix steered her through the Halls of Moria and through the archways toward the master staircase, walking backward the whole time.

Phoenix hit the first stair, and Mr. Greene and Sofia came up behind Aunt Beryl to assist. The two of them followed their tottering mistress up the stairs at a snail's pace, each placing a hand on Aunt Beryl's back to keep her from tumbling backward. Together they propelled her up the steps as Piper followed.

Once they were all at the top of the stairs, Phoenix pulled Aunt Beryl into her room, and he maneuvered around and gently helped her sit on the mattress. Piper was right there to help, lifting Aunt Beryl's dirty feet off the floor and covering her with the blanket.

The four of them left the bedroom, and Sofia pulled the door closed with a soft click.

Mr. Greene let out a breath and whispered, "She'll blame the dogs for the grass on her carpet in the morning." He clapped Phoenix lightly on the shoulder. "Thank you, young man. Your aunt hasn't been herself for many months, and it makes me happy to know we're all looking out for her well-being together." Then he smiled through his fatigue and said, "Excellent teamwork, everyone. I'll see you in the morning." He dipped his head slightly, and then he and Sofia headed back to their own apartments.

A few minutes later Piper tucked Phoenix into bed, and the boy was sound asleep before his sister left the room.

Piper snuggled back underneath the warm covers of her own bed and pulled out her diary.

Dear Dad, I wish you could tell me what Aunt Beryl was like before, like a long time ago. Was she mean and bossy? I guess she's not so much mean any more . . . she's just sorta there. I think if she smiles, her face might break or something.

I don't know. Maybe I should try to be nicer.

I guess she'll never know how Phoenix helped her back to bed with the whole sleepwalking thing. Oh well. I'm not telling her.

Moments before drifting off, she wondered how Phoenix knew Aunt Beryl was taking a midnight stroll in the first place.

He somehow knew about Mom's accident. It's no wonder he knew about Aunt Beryl too.

16

Peppermint Dreams

"My dreams are so lifelike," Darcy said.
"When I'm asleep here, it's like I'm alive in
another place, living someone else's story."
The Mage narrowed his eyes at her and said,
"Well, of course you are."
–Dana Schreiber

Water lapped softly at the sides of the yellow raft. Piper looked around, trying to focus on something, anything, beyond the edges, but there was only this blanket of ink.

"Phoenix?" she whispered, the darkness swallowing her words. "Where are you?"

He was here with her just a minute ago, because she could still smell the peanut butter. She recognized this yellow boat, and this place of water, and this insistent searching, but she couldn't put her finger on the memory.

What were we doing here last time?

It wasn't raining any longer, and the water was calm as the little boat rocked back and forth on the waves. Piper smelled salt water, and fish, and fresh ocean air along with . . .

Lavender and eucalyptus.

She breathed it in, as deep as she could get it, hoping to lock the fragrance and the memory inside her lungs and not wanting to exhale or let any of it out so that she could remember as long as possible.

Naomi always had lavender and eucalyptus lotion in her bag. After they were done swimming, Naomi would dry off and slather the lotion all over her arms and legs and shoulders to keep her skin soft. In the summertime she would wrap little Piper warm and sleepy and swim-tired in a fluffy beach towel. Piper would breathe in the soothing lavender-eucalyptus smell and fall asleep on her mother's lap while Gordon and Phoenix looked for shells near the water.

Phoenix and his father would run along the surf, and baby-toddler Phoenix would squeal and laugh when the water tickled his toes. Gordon would sweep Phoenix up with his solid-muscle arms and toss the boy into the air, catching him easily and spinning in a circle as the water splashed around them. Even if Piper was in a foul mood, she couldn't help but laugh right along with her baby brother because his laugh was contagious. *He* was contagious. His green-and-amber sparkling eyes shone from a light that flickered within, causing everyone who saw him to pause, and to look deeper, and to wonder what the child could see.

Piper heard him laughing now. Far away, deep in the darkness beyond where she could see from the yellow life raft, she could hear Phoenix laughing and splashing in the water, and his voice wasn't a three-year-old toddler voice. It was an older voice. It was a Now Voice. And Piper realized that the Now Voice wasn't alone, because she could just make out the rise and fall of another voice, deeper and stronger.

Where her mother was a cloud of lavender and eucalyptus, her father was a burst of strong peppermint candy coming in on a hot cup of black coffee. He always had one or the other with him, the scents mingling together and radiating strength and warmth. Piper weighed no more than a stuffed doll to Gordon. He would scoop her up with great tenderness and she would nestle down and melt into his solid, comforting chest to be carried to the car when the beach-tired sun began to set.

The lavender and eucalyptus faded away; the bracing aroma of peppermint took its place. As pieces and edges of words began to roll in toward Piper from across the water, she realized that Phoenix was listening to someone.

Piper needed to understand what the voice was saying. She leaned forward in the raft, straining to listen, willing her ears to translate and force the murky rise and fall of sounds to arrange themselves into words.

" *...ow...*"

Splashing. More laughter.

She leaned forward even more, and her elbow struck something hard that hadn't been there a moment ago. She looked down into the dark raft, and it took a few seconds for her eyes to adjust and identify what it was.

Oars.

" *...foun...*"

Gordon had been away for so long that Piper had almost forgotten how the peppermint smelled, how she could almost taste the spicy sweetness when he hugged her close and she breathed him in. The squeezing ache of worry in her chest began to lessen bit by bit as the strong peppermint aroma enveloped her and came to rest squarely in front of her nose.

"*I found it...*"

"Daddy?" she whispered. Piper reached out to take hold of the oars in the peppermint-scented air as the dream melted away and she woke up.

Piper didn't have a pocket deep enough to put her feelings in. The Darkness Where Mom was Not was still too real, too deep, and too close for her to even imagine seeing her father again after all this time, dreams or no dreams.

She pulled out her diary.

Dear Dad, will you stop coming into my dreams because it makes it too hard when I wake up and you're still not here. Don't know why I write in this thing, cause you're not gonna ever read it. You used to tell me to pray when I was scared of the dark as a little kid, but I forgot how.

Maybe Phoenix and I should take one of the dogs and run away like the Boxcar Children and live on our own.

Despite all Mr. Greene's talk about being close to God and *everywhen* and *thin* places, her heart felt empty, and her disbelief seemed full as she rolled over and cried herself to sleep.

17

Riddles in the Light

There are millions and billions and
trillions of words on pages in this world.
And still there is more to say that has not yet been said.
—Mary Alice Kelly

Piper awoke the next morning with a dull morning-after-crying headache, taking in the view of her still-not-quite-home bedroom in Aunt Beryl's house on the first day of May. The sun had just begun to rise, and she could see through the half-parted curtains that the sky was a chipper shade of blue. She rubbed the sleep from her eyes and rolled over to check the time. A new cipher note from Phoenix was propped up against her clock radio.

160-30-9, 48-10-4

Her paperback copy of *The Giver* was on the nightstand like always, and the poor book was beginning to show its age with soft, dog-eared corners and binding glue that was barely holding the pages together.

I need to get another copy of this book soon; hardback next time.

It didn't take long to decode her brother's message.

"found it"

Piper jumped from the bed, stepped into her slippers, and shrugged on her robe. She rushed to her brother's room only to find it empty. "Phoenix?" she called, her heart thumping with anticipation. "Phoenix!" she called, louder, looking down the empty hallways and peering over the balustrade.

What is this note supposed to mean?!

Even when I find him, he won't be able to explain it to me.

She shoved the note into the pocket of her robe and went back to her room, turning the peppermint dream over and over in her thoughts. As she gazed around the room absentmindedly, her eyes came to rest on me, still sitting unread on her shelf.

I wonder if that book, Novus Fabula, *is to blame for all of this.*

The aroma of bacon and pancakes wafted up the stairs, and Piper followed her nose down to find Sofia alone in the kitchen. Questions and riddles for Phoenix would have to wait.

"Morning, Sofia," Piper said as she sat down at the breakfast bar.

She smiled wide and said, "Good morning, Piper. I hope you're hungry!"

Piper nodded as her empty stomach growled in demand for food. The rich aroma helped wash away some of the sadness from the night before as she said, "It smells so good in here! Where is everybody?" She could see the remains of three other breakfast plates in the sink.

"Phoenix already ate and went outside with Quincy and the other two just now. I swear, it's like your little brother can speak Dog!" Sofia nodded in the direction of the back door as a strand of hair sprang loose from a bobby pin and bounced down in front of her eyes. "They're all the way down by the tree line."

Piper's eyes widened. "Has the mud hole dried up?" she asked, dreading another morning spent scrubbing gobs of sticky mud from all three dogs.

Sofia laughed. "Mr. Greene said we're in the clear."

"Oh, good!" Piper said. She took a sip of the orange juice Sofia had set on the breakfast bar and asked, "What about Aunt Beryl and Mr. Greene?"

"Mr. Greene had to drive your aunt down into Bangor for some meetings today, so the two of them headed out at the crack of dawn," she explained, placing a stack of pancakes and a side of crispy bacon in front of Piper. "They'll be back tomorrow."

Piper's mouth watered as she poured maple syrup over the steaming pancakes and plowed into them with her fork. "These are so good!" she said with her mouth stuffed full. "Everything you make is good!"

With a satisfied smile Sofia said, "I'm glad you think so! Phoenix ate two whole pancakes, and he tasted a little piece of bacon too." She started humming to herself as she cleaned up the breakfast dishes.

Between bites of bacon and pancakes, Piper asked, "Do you think sometimes dreams can be real? Like parts of them come true?"

"Oh, yes," she said. "No doubt about it, dreams can tell you things. Sometimes they're a bunch of nonsense, and you can blame the weirdo, skateboard-riding, polka dot dinosaur dreams on too much pizza before bed. Sometimes they're just plain scary, like nightmares, and yes, sometimes they can be like messages." She looked up at Piper and asked, "Did your dream say something to you last night?"

Piper nodded, swallowing down another huge bite of pancake with a sip of orange juice. "I think so. And Phoenix left me a note . . ."

Who is Sofia going to tell?

It would be nice to have someone to share my secret with.

"He doesn't talk out loud, you know," Piper said.

Sofia nodded, turning to the sink to scrub out a pan. "Right," she said. "But there's no doubt he talks to the dogs, and he has his way of communicating with people; especially with you."

"Yes, and he's been writing me these little notes, like the one you found in my pocket a while back. It's not a numbers game, actually. It's a code that he came up with, and every so often he'll write me something." Piper took another sip of juice and retrieved the latest note from the pocket of her robe. "Sometimes it's just normal stuff, and sometimes I don't understand what they mean, like this one. And then other times, it's like Phoenix knows things before they happen. Do you think people can know things before they happen?"

Sofia nodded as she wiped the counter and the stovetop with a wet cloth. "Absolutely," she said. "My gramma was that way. She'd have dreams about all sorts of stuff, and she would know things before they happened all the time. She always said it was a gift from God." Sofia rolled her eyes and added, "She didn't pass that gift down to me, and I'm not sure whether to be happy or sad about it!"

Piper dragged the last bite of pancake through the syrup and finished it off, patting her stomach with a smile. "I'm so full!"

Piper stared back at the note again, absentmindedly turning it over and over in her fingers and having no idea what the words meant, except that they had stepped right out of her dream. She gave up after a minute and shoved the paper back into her pocket. She watched Sofia pull out a cutting board to chop some onions and peppers, and the easy way she used the knife and hummed while she worked made Piper want to try it.

"Sofia, can you teach me to make something?" Piper asked. "It doesn't matter what it is; you can pick. Everything you make is so good, and I'm ready to learn how to cook."

Sofia came around beside Piper and wrapped her arm around the girl's shoulder, leaning in for a gentle squeeze. "I would *love* to teach you how to cook! I'm gonna teach you to make one of my favorites, chicken parmigiana. I'll make sure we have all the groceries we need, and we can make it for dinner one night this week."

Sofia hesitated and then leaned in toward Piper again. She sniffed the top of Piper's head with a puzzled smile on her face. "Did you have some kinda candy this morning?" she asked.

"Candy?" Piper repeated.

Sofia leaned closer and sniffed again, longer and more deeply. "You have some scented peppermint shampoo or something? I'm smelling peppermint, but sweet like a big piece of candy cane." She smoothed Piper's hair and said, "I like it!"

Piper stared at Sofia for a moment, not comprehending. Then she looked at the note from Phoenix in her hand and read it again.

"found it"

Piper's thoughts went back to that morning's life raft dream, remembering the muddled deep voice breaking through, and splashes, and laughter, and the overpowering aroma of peppermint, and something that sounded an awful lot like her father's voice.

"I found it . . ."

Piper couldn't begin to find logical words to explain the reason that her hair smelled like peppermint, so she nodded. "Yes," she lied. Sofia patted Piper's shoulder and went back to chopping the vegetables.

Aunt Beryl wasn't home to fuss, so Piper ran upstairs to her room. She dressed in a hurry and took a second to grab a handful of hair, pull it forward under her nose, and take a long sniff.

Smells like regular hair.

She swallowed hard and grabbed me from her nightstand with trembling hands. A pale blue light began to glow between her fingers, and a rush of fear made her shove me back onto the shelf.

I called her name with as much tenderness as I could muster. **Piper.**

She paused.

Wait. Phoenix read it, and he didn't turn into a weasel or anything. If he can read it, so can I.

She squared her shoulders and pulled me from the shelf as intrigue became louder than fear.

Hello, Dearest Piper. I'm so glad you're ready to hear your Story.

Piper was becoming more certain by the moment that her dream and her brother's cipher notes were connected to me somehow, and that we were trying to tell her something.

It was time for Piper to find out what it was.

18

Between Heaven and Earth

Surely the author must have felt the power in his fingertips when he grasped the quill. I should think his hands still tremble with it a thousand years hence.
—Ann Eliza Matthews

An early warm spell had rendered the frigid Maine spring a little more bearable during the last few days, and Piper felt her spirits lift when she thought about clear skies and warmer temperatures. Dressed in her Atlanta Falcons hoodie, she shoved me into her backpack along with an apple, a granola bar, and a bottle of water. Then she marched out the back door with questions swirling inside her head.

Who found what?

Was that really Dad's voice I heard out there in the water?

How did a scent from my dream make its way into my hair so that Sofia could smell it? That makes NO sense!

Another thought made her pause and glance back at the house.

Is it because Sofia can hear the whispering book too?

As she made her way down past the manicured garden toward the big corner tree Mr. Greene had called "a thin place," Piper turned the words from her brother's note over and over again in her head.

"Found it."

If it was Dad in the dream and Dad in this note, what did he find?

How did Phoenix know about Mom and going into the Light beforehand? And how does he know about Dad, if it is Dad? Can Phoenix hear Dad talking to him? Did he have a yellow life raft dream like I did? Did he smell the peppermint too?

There were too many questions that were too big for Piper to wrap her brain around, so she shook her head and willed them all to go away. She reached the end of the low wall that surrounded the formal garden area and turned right to follow the eastern edge. A greening lawn spread out in front of her, the grass having started to respond to the warmer temperatures.

Piper had wanted to climb the tree to seek out the ocean view that Mr. Greene had told them about their first day here, but each time she had tried, she couldn't figure out where to put her feet. The lowest branch was out of reach, and the fat tree trunk didn't seem to have any clear footholds. She refused to ask for help from anyone, wanting to conquer the climb all by herself.

Piper set her jaw and tightened the straps of the backpack to both shoulders, determined to make it up into the tree. She tried to jump up to touch the lowest branch four times, becoming more frustrated with every miss.

She noticed a knobby collection of bark protruding out of one side of the trunk two feet off the ground, and it looked wide enough to serve as a step. She leaned in, trying to wrap her arms around the tree trunk as she put all her weight on the knobby step and hoisted herself up.

Piper stood suspended there for five seconds, trying to figure out her next move as she pressed her body into the tree. Then her shoe slipped.

The craggy, rigid bark of the tree dug hard into her cheek and shoulder and wrists and ankles all at once as she slipped and landed unceremoniously on the ground. It was only a two-foot drop, but it may as well have been twenty.

She curled up into a little ball and began to sob.

Dad would have been here to boost me up.

Dad would have caught me if I fell.

Seeing her father's blurry, hard-to-recall face in her mind made Piper cry even harder, so hard that her stomach began to ache as the muscles tied up in knots. Though she pretended That Stuff didn't listen to her anymore, she let loose in her thoughts and finally gave a voice to the pent-up feelings screaming to be let out of her heart.

Where are You, God? Can You even hear me? Do You even care about me down here?

What did I do to deserve this?

Why did you make it so stormy that night that Mom's car went off the road? You could have stopped it!

Where is Dad? Why did You let him be taken? Is he hurt? Is he even alive? It's not FAIR!

Why did You leave me here all alone with an old lady who doesn't like me? I can't do this by myself! Phoenix needs me to look after him, but I can't be Mom's replacement. I'm just a kid!

Mr. Greene said this tree is closer to You, and I can't even get up there!

IT'S NOT FAIR!

After a long bout of sobbing, Piper felt a cool breeze lift her hair. She opened her eyes and sat up, brushing twigs and sticks and dirt from her tear-streaked face and neck. She sniffed and looked up into the tree in disbelief at what she saw.

A hand she recognized was reaching down from the lowest branch.

"Phoenix?" she said as she stared, blinking and bewildered. "How . . . ?" She scrambled to her feet and dusted off her jeans. Then she made sure both backpack straps were squarely on her shoulders before reaching up to grab her brother's hand.

He was far stronger than she expected. In an instant Piper was up on the lowest branch of the tree beside her brother. Then Phoenix jumped down out of the tree and ran off, leaving Piper to her thoughts.

"You have to show me how you got up here!" she called after him.

Piper surveyed her new surroundings. Above her she saw that one of the upper branches ran sideways at a right angle to the main trunk, making a perfect chair-like shape. She climbed to it easily, then relaxed against the tree and stretched out her legs with no fear of falling.

She heard Mr. Greene's voice in her head saying, "It's easier to sense the presence of God when you're in a thin place."

I can tell you, Dear Reader, that Mr. Greene is not wrong about this. My spine tingled, the ink within me sharpened, and the words that I had to share with Piper Guthrie began to well up inside my pages and seep into the air with a swirling, pale blue light.

There had never been a time prior to this when Piper had been nervous to read a book, but I could feel her heart fluttering as she ran her hand across my cover. She had read plenty of stories in the past, too many to remember, but not a single one had glowed with its own light or whispered to her beforehand. But now she was ready to hear it.

19

A Day in a Tree

*My heart is stirred by a noble theme as I
recite my verses for the king; my tongue
is the pen of a skillful writer.*
—The Sons of Korah, Psalm 45:1 NIV

We're in a tree now. Breezy; leafy; fresh; birdsong; earth and sky. Close your eyes, Dear Reader, and picture it. Need a snack? How about a water bottle? Settle in for a story. Careful now; don't tumble out.

Piper opened the front cover and flipped past the title page, her heart singing with anticipation as my greeting poured forth. The whispers grew louder, flowing from inside the pages and wrapping themselves around my Reader as I let the binding exhale, opening my secrets and suffusing the tree with light. As the mystery of the whispers drew her in, Piper found herself falling slowly down the rabbit hole with Alice, tumbling head over heels and further into familiar strangeness with every word and every page and every chapter that she read.

You see, Dear Reader, I already knew her story. It's the one she needed to tell, the very same one she needed to read with new eyes, to hear with new ears.

Every single thing in the world that Piper loved was woven in and throughout the story. Her tongue knew the taste of the main character's favorite hot peppermint tea in winter. She recognized the candy-sweet scent of Virginia bluebells, picking them by the armload next to a quiet stream in the springtime. Piper nodded in understanding when the character struggled to fit in at school, where even the teachers thought her odd and standoffish, and all she wanted to do was punch the bullies in the teeth and climb to the roof and read another book so she didn't have to *feel* so much.

Warm spring sunshine filled the dappled spaces between the budding leaves. She sat motionless, reading, oblivious to the chirping of birds and the fact that lunchtime had approached and then was gone.

Piper and I were alone in the thin place of the reading tree. It didn't matter that she started to cry when the main character's life became confusing and different from the lives of her friends and classmates after her little brother's doctor said some big-sounding words that she didn't understand. My heart ached right along with Piper's with love for a little brother who once squealed and laughed and spoke and then became locked in a world of mute silence. The longing to know and be known by him, her brother and best friend, was heavy for such a little girl. My words gave speech to Piper's confusion, teaching her that it was okay to feel angry and disappointed, giving her a voice where she felt she had none. And when a group of neighborhood boys called the little brother a retarded freak, Piper laughed out loud when the story's character exacted her revenge against them by painting their bicycles bubblegum pink.

Then came the first of the darkest parts. I believe, Dear Reader, that Piper almost closed the book when the father in the story disappeared in the jungle. She was more familiar with the character's sadness and anger and fear than she ever wanted to be. Somehow it was okay here and now to let those bottled up tears fall where they would from her place high up in the reading tree. Piper cried in solidarity for the brave girl in the story who pushed through and kept going without her father. And Piper's heart exploded with relief when the mother in the story woke up one day and wasn't crying anymore, but resumed brushing her hair and brushing her teeth and cooking breakfast and kissing foreheads. My story didn't erase the Not Knowing, but there was an agreement, a deciding *not* to give up hope that her father would somehow find his way back home. I felt Piper latch onto this dogged resolve as she found her own fragile hope rising.

Piper stopped reading when she realized the Biggest Darkness was coming up next in the story, the Darkness Where Mom Was Not.

Would you have continued on, Dear Reader?

Piper thought long and hard about closing the book and not reading any more of it, but that wasn't possible. So she drank some water and ate an apple and a chewy chocolate chip granola bar. She launched the apple core as far out into the grass as she could, took a deep breath, and found enough bravery to keep reading.

All of the grown-ups were so quiet and awkward, taken to whispering around the children when their mother died, acting like none of them knew what they were supposed to say. To Piper, it felt like being set adrift in a boat with no anchor, no oars, no current, and no captain. Somehow Piper was just expected to be her own captain, but no one had taught her what a captain was supposed to do, and she didn't have a map or a compass or lessons on how to sail. Naomi was both captain and compass for Piper and Phoenix, and now Mom Was Not.

Hot tears of relief flooded her eyes as the story gave her words to acknowledge just how much it hurt to have a piece of her torn out. Even if this girl was just a character in a book, she understood Piper in a way that no one else could.

Her heart swelled in admiration for the character's resolve. She was brave in the doing of everyday things like dishes and homework and tying her little brother's shoes and answering a phone that rang far too often. She wasn't the least bit angry at her brother for being different. They had a tightly woven knot of friendship that nothing could untie.

The girl in the story prayed, real prayers, *out loud*, and she never acted like those prayers just stopped at the ceiling. She acted like God was with her everywhere, and everywhen, ceiling or no ceiling, parents or no parents, a Being who heard every word she said and made her believe that she mattered.

In a flash, Piper's understanding opened up, and she saw the yellow life raft dreams for what they were: she was being carried. Even though it was dark and stormy around her, she wasn't going to drown. She longed to be with her mother and father, but here in this thin place, she was overcome with an unexplainable peace that could only come from God.

The book didn't have a happily-ever-after ending, like the kinds of stories that pretend all the dark things were just a dream and the characters wake up and everyone is alive and there is cake and rainbows and kissing. If it had ended that way, Dear Reader, I'm sure that Piper would have done what Aunt Beryl wanted to do and auctioned me off to the highest bidder.

The girl in the story didn't pretend that every hard thing had some lesson behind it, or that life could be tied up in a neat little bow. The story I gave Piper left her satisfied, and perplexed, and tearful, and exhausted, and full of more questions than answers. A glimmer of hope had awakened in her soul, and my last words left her filled with a belief in the importance of her own unfolding story.

Piper blinked as she turned my last page, not realizing that the sun had begun to set and the sky barely offered enough light for her to read. As she leaned over the branches to see about getting down, she was surprised and not surprised to see Phoenix sitting in the grass beneath her, leaning against the tree with all three dogs asleep in a circle around him. She didn't realize three big dogs could be that quiet, but the Dog Whisperer was in their midst.

"Look out below!" Piper called down, starting to descend.

Phoenix and the dogs made way for Piper as she jumped easily to the grass. She was thankful that Phoenix didn't need her to say anything because her words would have failed her. She took her brother's hand, and they walked toward the house in the waning light. Piper glanced back at the reading tree as Mr. Greene's voice came back to her once again.

Heaven and earth are normally about three feet apart, but when you're in a thin place, heaven is much closer.

20

Baffling Questions

The volumes stood on the shelves, resolute, silent as
sentries with unfired weapons at the ready.
— Adeliza Livingston

Sofia didn't seem the least bit put out that the children hadn't bothered to show up for lunch or dinner. She had kept two plates of spaghetti and meatballs and thick garlic bread warm in the oven for supper, and she nodded with appreciation as Phoenix and Piper devoured every last noodle. "It's good for you two to play outside all day," she said. "So much better for you than staying cooped up in your room."

The emotional roller coaster Piper had ridden that day had worn her out. After dinner she went straight to bed and slept a peaceful, dreamless sleep.

Out of habit she woke up at the usual time for breakfast the next morning, even though Aunt Beryl wasn't there to notice if the children were on schedule. Piper was ushered into the kitchen by the aroma of cinnamon rolls and sausage. Phoenix was sitting at the breakfast counter already, sipping some hot chocolate and watching Sofia with something close to interest. Piper put an arm around her brother and said, "Good morning, little brother." For a moment he leaned into his sister and rested his head against her shoulder, and a lump rose in Piper's throat at the unexpected hint of affection. Then the cinnamon rolls with loads of melting icing appeared, and Phoenix launched into his breakfast with a peanut butter sandwich in one hand and a cinnamon roll in the other.

Quincy, Lincoln, and Teddy all thumped their tails at Piper in unison, but none of them left their posts at her brother's feet. "The Dog Whisperer and his minions," Piper said as she patted each dog's head and sat on the stool beside Phoenix.

Sofia nodded toward Phoenix as she offered Piper a mug of hot peppermint tea. "Mum's the word, but somebody had a little slumber party in his bedroom last night," she said with a wry smile. "I went to go put the dogs in their crates, and they refused to come when I called them, so I went looking and found all three of them on his bed, pretending they couldn't hear me." She shrugged. "Phoenix was happy, the dogs were happy; it's okay by me!"

"Auntie's away and the dogs will play!" Piper said.

Piper had her fill of the luscious cinnamon rolls and the savory sausage, questions building up inside of her head while she ate. The more she thought about the story I had given her yesterday, the bigger her questions became.

After breakfast Piper looked out the window and saw another clear sky that promised warm temperatures. "Phoenix, let's take the dogs outside to play again, okay?" She smiled at Sofia. "We'll come in for lunch this time, though; promise!" Piper grabbed a couple of granola bars from the cabinet and added them to her book-filled backpack before hoisting it over her shoulder.

Sofia waved them off as she cleared the dishes. "Bah! Go play! You both look bright eyed and bushy-tailed after being outside all day yesterday, and it's nice to see a little color in your cheeks."

Over the last several years, Piper had grown used to the way Phoenix made his way through the world. Occasionally he would look at his surroundings as he walked beside his family, but often his expression was either vacant or frustrated. Sometimes when they were outside on a warm day, he would turn his face up toward the sun and close his eyes. It was one of the few times Piper could tell he was enjoying himself.

Phoenix was different today. His face was different, and his sparkling eyes were different, greener and brighter today than Piper had ever seen them. No one else may have been able to tell, but Piper knew that her brother had lost some of that vacant look. He still didn't say anything, but there was more of Phoenix inside of Phoenix. Piper wondered if her little brother had been as affected as deeply as she was when he'd finished reading the story I'd given him.

Piper stopped short as she realized something.

Wait. The book wasn't about him. It was about me. Why would Phoenix be so interested in a story that's all about his sister?

Piper and Phoenix walked all the way to the end of the formal garden and sat down on the low wall near the corner. Phoenix looked out toward the woods, absentmindedly tugging on Quincy's ear.

"I read the book," Piper said. "I know you liked it just as much as I did, and I want to ask you about it because it all seems so weird and it doesn't make any sense." Piper pulled me from the backpack and set me on her lap, running her palm over the cover.

"What was the book about, Phoenix?"

He stopped petting Quincy and reached into the pocket of his jeans and pulled out a tiny scrap of paper. At first Piper thought her brother would produce a pen and write a ciphered answer to her question. Instead he came over and stood in front of her, looking hard into her eyes with his knees touching hers. He took Piper's hand, pressed the little paper into her palm, and folded her fingers over it with a gentle squeeze. Then he spun around and began running toward the tree line with the dogs in close pursuit.

Piper retrieved *The Giver* from her backpack, unfolded the note, and read the single set of numbers Phoenix had written.

11-4-4

She decoded it.

The note simply said, "me."

Wait.

He says the story was about HIM?

How did Phoenix know ahead of time that I was going to ask him that question?

Piper tried to approach this evolving mystery logically, recalling all of the puzzle pieces and trying to assemble them in her head. But not all things can be answered with simple logic. I wonder, Dear Reader, if you might agree.

Piper began to have an internal argument. A "what if" began niggling in her thoughts.

Novus Fabula. *That's Latin for "New Story."*

What if Phoenix read a different book than the one I read?

That's not possible. Books don't change. They can't change.

But what if they could?

So it's a "new" story, as in new every time someone new reads it? How is that even possible?

The rumble of car tires crunching on gravel sounded from the driveway. Piper remembered that Mr. Greene and Aunt Beryl were supposed to return from their trip into the city that morning. She returned her things to the backpack and tossed it over her shoulder as she headed for the house with determination. Piper had decided, Dear Reader, to enlist the help of her guide. After all, he is the one who knew about the "thin place." If anyone could help figure out this mystery, it would be Original Greene.

Piper came around the side of the house just as Aunt Beryl disappeared into the front door. Mr. Greene was still unloading the bags from the car. "Good morning, Piper," he said with a broad smile. "Did you and Sofia and Phoenix get along all right while we were gone?" His eyes twinkled. "Not too much mischief, I hope."

She followed him into the house and through the entryway where he set the bags on the floor. "No mischief," Piper said. "We managed to avoid caking the dogs with mud, but I hear they ditched their crates for a sleepover with Phoenix last night."

Mr. Greene laughed, shaking his head.

Piper wasn't sure how to phrase her questions about smelling peppermint in her dreams, Phoenix seeing the future, and books that glowed and whispered from library shelves. She figured Mr. Greene would think she had lost her marbles. "I have something to ask you though, later, when you have time," she said.

He nodded. "Certainly. I had planned to get started on those bookshelves in your room today, so once I get the car unloaded, we can get to work and you can ask me then. Deal?"

Piper gave him a fast hug. "Yes!" she said, reminding herself not to jump up and down because Aunt Beryl was home now. "Yes! Deal!"

She looked up and saw Aunt Beryl watching her from the top of the stairs with her arms crossed and a puzzled expression on her face.

Mom would expect me to be nice to her, even though she doesn't really deserve it.

Piper returned her aunt's steady gaze with a sincere smile. "Good morning, Aunt Beryl," she ventured, hoping she didn't sound like she had practiced a speech. "How was your trip to Bangor?"

Mr. Greene made his way up the stairs with the suitcases as Aunt Beryl said, "It was quite profitable; thank you for asking." She hesitated, clearing her throat. "I hope you and Phoenix behaved yourselves."

Piper nodded and said, "We played outside with the dogs most of the day." She didn't dare mention that the dogs had played hooky from their crates, because she wasn't sure how Aunt Beryl might feel about dog fur on the bed linens.

"Good," Aunt Beryl said. Just then the telephone began to ring from inside her study and Aunt Beryl nodded curtly. "See you at lunch, then," she said, retreating down the hall. Piper heard her aunt answer the phone and then close the study door.

Mr. Greene came back downstairs and patted Piper's shoulder as he walked by. "Give her time," he suggested. "I think she's starting to warm up to you."

"Coulda fooled me," Piper mumbled.

Piper tried to imagine how her mom would be acting if two distant relatives were suddenly thrust into their little house in Atlanta and made part of their family. Naomi was big on hugging, and Piper knew without a doubt that hugs would have been handed out frequently and with gusto. With a pang in her belly, Piper realized how desperately she longed for a good, old-fashioned bear hug from someone who loved her.

21

Theories on Magic

"A story?" the dragon echoed with a smoky chuckle.
"I suppose I could tell you just one
before I turn you into toast."
–Gualterius Falsus, "The Tale of Mendax the Mede"

Mr. Greene disassembled the empty bookcases that were in the basement, as they would have been too large to fit through the doorways intact. Piper helped him carry each wooden piece up two flights of stairs and into her room, and the muscles in her legs were spent by the time all the pieces were on the bedroom floor. She sat on her bed and watched Mr. Greene begin to put the bookcases back together with a cordless drill and a screwdriver.

"Okay, so what was it that you wanted to ask me?" he asked.

Piper decided it was just too weird to try to explain about smelling her father's peppermint candy in a dream, or Phoenix knowing things, or books you could hear from across the room. So she started with a normal-sounding question. "You know all those books that were in my uncle's library that we boxed up? Where did they come from?"

"They're from hundreds of shops, big and small, all over the world," said Mr. Greene. "Your uncle's passion was collecting antiques and first editions and rare copies. According to your aunt, Lonnie would spend hours at estate sales and auctions and second-hand bookstores. He was strict about keeping records, and the folder with all of his receipts is downstairs in the basement in the black filing cabinet beside the stairs. Each time I located and purchased a book that was on his list, I put the receipt in that folder. Why do you ask?"

Here goes.

Piper swallowed hard. "Phoenix borrowed one of the books before you and I boxed them all up," she said. "Sorry."

Mr. Greene smiled. "Borrowing priceless books from the library you weren't permitted to enter?" he teased. "Don't worry, I won't rat on you for jumping the gun."

"Thanks," said Piper sheepishly. "Anyway, Phoenix stayed up all night reading the book he borrowed, and then he gave it to me with this little note that he wrote, telling me that it *wanted* to be read. So I read it, and . . ."

There was no way Piper could hide her confusion, and Mr. Greene set the screwdriver down for a second. "And what?" he asked, concerned. "Did the story frighten you somehow?"

"Oh, no. Not at all," she said. "It's just so hard to explain, but there is something . . . *different* about this book."

Piper reached into her backpack and pulled me onto her lap. She had expected to hear me whispering as I came out of hiding, but I had grown silent for her. She offered me to Mr. Greene. "Here."

Dear Reader, I cannot tell you how my spine tingles when I am passed along and shared! I think perhaps every book must feel this way, especially when being passed on to a Reader like Mr. Greene.

He reached out and took me carefully into his hands, his face a giant question mark. "Different how?" he asked, running his hands along the spine and the front cover as he squinted at the title. "*Novus Fabula*," he recited. "I'm a little rusty on my Latin," he said with a wry smile.

"Oh, don't worry," Piper said. "The story's not in Latin; just the title. I looked it up in my uncle's Oxford dictionary, and it means 'New Story.' You don't know where Uncle Lonnie found this?" she asked.

"I sure don't," he said. "Don't believe I've ever noticed this in the library before. But there were so many books in there, I could have just missed it."

"Phoenix read it first, and then I read it, and when I was done I asked him to tell me what it was about," she explained.

"Was he able to answer you?" Mr. Greene asked, surprised.

"Not with regular talking," she said. "Phoenix writes me these little notes in this code that he made up, so that's how he can answer me. And from what he wrote, from what *he* said the book was about, I think the book . . . This sounds so weird, but I think the book *changed*."

Confusion and intrigue were on Mr. Greene's face as he asked, "Changed? How do you mean?"

Piper shrugged. "The book I read was about me, like it was written just for *me*. But when I asked Phoenix, he said the book was about *him*. We can't both be right, can we?"

"Oh, I see," said Mr. Greene with a nod. "And he told you the book *wants* to be read?"

Piper nodded. "It was like we could hear it talking to us from the day we got here, and Phoenix figured out what it was trying to say first."

"So now you'd like me to test your theory," he said. "If I read the book and it's about you and Phoenix, then there's no mystery. But if I read it and it's a book about me, then we can assume there's some kind of magic happening in it."

Piper frowned, hoping Mr. Greene wasn't making fun. "Do you think that's stupid?" she asked. "Magic books?"

Mr. Greene picked up the screwdriver again and got back to work on the bookcase assembly. "Will you hold this piece up for me, like this?" he asked. "I need another hand."

Piper jumped from the bed and held the piece as steady as she could while Mr. Greene put the screws in place. "To answer your question, I think there are things in this world that not everybody always understands. I also think the Big Man sometimes gets our attention in ways we don't expect."

Piper cocked her head sideways. "The Big Man? You mean God?"

Mr. Greene nodded solemnly. "That's right," he answered, looking straight at Piper. "I was always taught that God is bigger than I can imagine. So I would never say that God can't reach inside the words we read in a book or a song and tell us things we need to hear."

"You think this book is something like that?" Piper asked.

Mr. Greene shrugged and said, "Why not? Every time I walk to the edge of the ocean, I close my eyes and listen to the waves rolling in, because the ocean speaks. To those who have ears to hear, to those few people who find the time to *really* listen, things in this world are constantly speaking."

"I never thought of it that way," Piper admitted.

"Who's to say God wouldn't be able to take common, everyday things and change them somehow, turning them into a thought or a feeling or a message that only the smallest handful of humans can understand? Such things aren't only possible, I believe they're more common than any of us realize. But if we try to talk about them out loud with just anybody, the nice people in white coats may put us in a padded room."

Piper laughed and handed Mr. Greene the next shelf. "You got that right!" she said

"You know," Mr. Greene continued, "God caused some pretty weird stuff to happen in Bible times, like when He made a donkey speak, or when He made a magic hand appear out of thin air and write on a wall to send a warning to a king."

Piper's mouth dropped open. "What? I don't remember hearing about those stories in Sunday school," she said.

"The talking donkey is in the book of Numbers, and the hand that writes on the wall is in the book of Daniel," he explained as he continued to work on the bookshelves. "And I bet some of the people who lived through those events would have called it 'magic' at the time, even though we know now that it was God Himself who caused those things to happen. I'm convinced that if God would do strange things like that thousands of years ago, He still does strange things like that today. Not everyone will agree with me, but that's okay. I think God is far too big to be kept in a box made with my tiny imagination."

Piper laughed. "So you'll read it? And then tell me what it was about?" she asked.

Mr. Greene smiled and placed me on top of Piper's dresser near the door before starting back on the shelf assembly. "Scout's honor," he said. "It'll be a few days before I can get started, though, because of my schedule, but I will read it." Leaning toward Piper with a conspiratorial smile he whispered, "I rather hope it *is* a magic book; can't say that I've ever read one."

22

The Unboxing

Too many books? That's like saying you've
got too many friends. It's preposterous!
—Alfred Doddle

In no time at all, the bookcases were assembled and standing ready to receive Piper's beloved collection. Two full walls were given over to shelving from floor to ceiling, and Piper smiled so hard that her cheeks were starting to ache as they brought the last of her book boxes up from the basement.

Phoenix came into the bedroom just then. "Hey, there!" Piper said. "Look! My books aren't downstairs in jail anymore!"

Phoenix stepped around the boxes, looking at the empty shelves that were waiting to become home to his sister's prized possessions. Then he reached into the box Piper had just opened, grabbed the first book he touched, and sat down on Piper's bed to read *Eragon*.

Are you familiar with the tale of *Eragon*, Dear Reader? Saphira is such a lovely dragon, and she was so careful not to breathe on me and accidentally singe my pages. We companions of the page look out for one another, you know.

Mr. Greene folded up his long legs and sat next to Piper on the floor to help. "Do you have your books arranged into any sort of system?" he asked, opening a box.

"Alphabetical by author's last name, of course," she replied, "as it should be with fiction."

He nodded. "Very good. If you agree, we'll start over on the left shelf with A at the top, then end on the right shelf with Z on the bottom. I would imagine you would enjoy shelving them yourself?"

Piper grinned and said, "Of course!"

Dear Reader, you may recognize a few of the wonderful titles Piper has collected over the years. Each one is a work of art unto itself, tales with which I would be happy to share a shelf.

Rediscovering each book was like saying hello to an old friend, and Piper was flooded with memories of the times and places she had received each one. "Oh, *The Secret Garden*," she said, stroking the cover. "Found this hardback at a thrift store for a dollar!" She put it on the floor near where she thought it should go and asked Mr. Greene, "You said your mother was a librarian. I guess you read a lot as a kid?"

He nodded. "I wore my mother out asking if the shipment of new arrivals had come in each month," he said. "Ah, here's *Little House on the Prairie*. A classic."

"No offense to the author, but this isn't one of my favorites," Piper said.

"How so?" Mr. Greene asked.

She explained, "Well, it's like this. *The Secret Garden* is a kid's book too, a lot like *Little House*. *The Secret Garden* talks all about being nice to people and not being bossy or rude, but does it in a way that makes you want to be kind to people, and leaves you feeling happy inside. The writer in *Little House* sounded like some crabby old grandma telling the reader how to behave. Things like, 'Children are to be seen and not heard,' or, 'That wasn't ladylike.' I mean, after Laura's dog gets swept away in the flooded river she says, 'I knew it was shameful to cry.' Who would ever say that?!"

Mr. Greene laughed. "Those are valid points. But why hold on to a book you don't love?"

Piper shrugged. "I don't know. I guess it's just so famous that I like having it. And I never know when I'll do a book report at school and need my own copy. Or maybe I'll join a book club and we'll read it because it's so famous."

"That makes sense," he said. "I suppose in any book club, some readers don't like certain books, but they can still be friends. I'm a huge fan of the *Little House* books, myself. They let me see how hard life was back then, and you get to see how people thought about things so differently than we do today."

Piper accepted his argument and set the book on the shelf.

As Mr. Greene unboxed another handful of books, he said, "Oh, *The Miraculous Journey of Edward Tulane*. I bought a copy of this one for my niece. Wonderful story."

I am honored to say, Dear Reader, that Edward Tulane himself is also a personal friend of mine. A quiet, solid, likeable fellow, despite the cotton stuffing between his ears.

Piper said, "See that stuffed bunny on my bed? It was a birthday present, given to me all boxed up with the *Edward Tulane* book."

"So your stuffed bunny's name is Edward, then?" Mr. Greene asked.

Piper rolled her eyes and said, "No way. Edward is way too common. I named him Farthfigery, that weird word the old lady uses in the book. Much more interesting!"

Mr. Greene laughed heartily as he placed the books near the bookcase. "Excellent choice," he said. He stopped, thinking for a moment. "What do you think about loaning a few of these books to Sofia?" he asked. "She wants to try to read more, but it's hard for her."

"What do you mean, it's hard for her?" Piper asked. "Like, not enough time in the day?"

Mr. Greene said, "I guess it's not something she goes around telling people, but I'm sure she's fine with you knowing. She has dyslexia. Do you know what that is?"

"Yep," Piper replied. "My friend Gabriella back in Atlanta has that same thing. She's really good at math, but she *hates* reading. I used to read a lot of my books out loud to her when she came for sleepovers, and she really liked that."

Mr. Greene nodded. "I did some research at the library in town and found some strategies to help Sofia improve her reading skills. She's been reading children's books to practice, and I'm sure she'd love some of these."

He cocked his head sideways and said, "You know, I think your love for books is one of the reasons your aunt has found it so hard to warm up to you."

"Why?" Piper asked. "She doesn't like books?"

"No, no. It's not that," he said. "She reads every night, but never the books from your uncle's library. She only reads the newest releases, brand new books delivered by mail once a month."

"Brand new books are good too," Piper said as she continued to unpack and sort. "Every book is brand new once."

Mr. Greene said, "That's true! I believe that every time she saw the collection that Lonnie loved so much, it reminded her that he wasn't here anymore. She blamed the books, in a way, because he was on a book buying trip in Italy when he died in a freak accident."

"What happened?" Piper whispered.

Mr. Greene shrugged and said, "He was searching for a certain book inside a tiny used bookstore in Rome. There was a natural gas explosion inside the shop, and your uncle and the shop owner were killed."

"Oh, wow, I didn't know that," Piper said, feeling sorry for her aunt. "Do you know why she decided to get rid of all my uncle's books after all this time?"

"Not exactly," said Mr. Greene. "But she called the design company the same day she received word of your arrival, saying something about a clean slate."

"Oh!" exclaimed Mr. Greene as he opened another box. "*Bridge to Terabithia*," he said. "My mother adored this story!"

"I threw that book across the room when I got to the end of chapter ten," Piper admitted. "But of course, I picked it back up and finished it, and then I re-read it like eight times. But I always wondered—when Leslie gave all her books to Jess—what kind of books a girl like Leslie would have in her library."

"Oh, my goodness, I haven't thought about this story in years," said Mr. Greene as he sat cross-legged on the floor and opened a shabby paperback. "*Wind in the Willows*."

"That book got me in trouble!" Piper exclaimed.

Mr. Greene said, "Let me guess. You were reading in school when you should have been listening to social studies or doing math."

"Nope!" she said. "Library; fourth grade. I had just finished it, and this boy was goofing off throwing spitballs at the bookshelves, so I called him a name I had read in that book."

Mr. Greene threw his head back and belly-laughed. "You didn't!"

"Yeah, I'm not proud of it. I just figured we'd be allowed to say the words that were in a book if it was in the school library, but apparently not!" she said. "Got sent to the principal. When I showed her the page where the word in the book was used, she said I could go back to class if I promised not to say that word again. She was laughing just like you are right now."

Mr. Greene stood and looked around the room. "Well, you'll have to suggest a couple of books you think Sofia would like."

Piper looked around and picked two books from the piles. "How about these? There's *The Wonderful Wizard of Oz* and *Because of Winn Dixie*."

Mr. Greene took Piper's copy of *The Wonderful Wizard of Oz* and opened up the front cover. Glancing at the first page, he asked, "What's this?" Squinting his eyes, he read the inscription scribbled in a childish, nearly illegible cursive handwriting. "It says here, '*Property Of Piper Bernadette Guthrie. Do Not Read Or Else.*'"

"Let me see that!" Piper said, grabbing the book from his hand to look at the lopsided scribble. "I have no memory of writing this." She shook her head and handed him the book. "I was a selfish little book-miser back then!"

He laughed. "It's hard to believe *Wizard of Oz* was published in 1900," said Mr. Greene as he thumbed through the pages. "I guess some stories are written so perfectly that they're destined to live forever."

Piper looked over at me sitting on the dresser, waiting to take my next Reader, Mr. Greene, under my spell. She wondered if I was one of those forever books.

Time will tell, Dear Reader.

23

Echo Chamber Trespass

Some books should be tasted, some devoured, but only a few should be chewed and digested thoroughly.
—Francis Bacon

Piper opened her eyes to an annoying beeping coming from outside her bedroom window. She blinked in the brightness of the morning and glanced at the clock. 6:15.

Who makes deliveries at sunrise?

She stumbled out of bed and pulled back the curtain to see who she should blame for waking her so early. There were four white delivery trucks in a line at the front door, all emblazoned with "Francesca's White Linen Catering" on the side. The day of Aunt Beryl's annual spring banquet had arrived.

Great. A bunch of old rich people I don't know.

Piper crawled back beneath the covers and smashed a pillow over her head with hopes of going back to sleep. But she heard several not-so-quiet voices and what sounded like a Bigfoot convention parading through the house beneath her, so she rolled out of bed with a groan. She made herself presentable for public viewing and headed down the service stairs to the kitchen.

A kettle of hot water was on the stove, and Piper helped herself to a cup of peppermint tea with extra sugar. Sofia had prepped a breakfast casserole the night before, and it was sitting on the breakfast bar wrapped up, piping hot and untouched.

Phoenix came downstairs into the kitchen as Piper was serving up her plate, so she pulled out the plate of peanut butter sandwiches Sofia had left in the fridge. "Hey, buddy," she said. "We'll have to lay low today. Aunt Beryl's banquet is tonight, and I bet she expects us to be invisible. Maybe we can hide out in my room and watch some old movies on my laptop."

The breakfast casserole was amazing, like everything else Sofia made. It had savory sausage, rich cheese, and torn up bits of buttery croissants all baked together with eggs like a quiche. Piper cleaned her plate and helped herself to seconds, and Phoenix even tried a few bites of it before Piper tidied up the kitchen.

The fresh-smelling breeze blowing down the hallway told Piper that the front door had been open for a while to admit the flood of catering staff. She didn't want to get in the caterers' way, but she wanted to see what all the banging was about. She took her brother's hand and went from the breakfast room around through the Echo Chamber to stand in the entrance to the Halls of Moria.

She counted eight people setting up and decorating tall cocktail tables that were scattered throughout the giant room. Each little table was covered with a floor-length white cloth that was gathered in the center halfway to the ground, and a floating candle in a fat round vase was set on top of each, to be lit during the party that evening. Greenery and potted plants and bright bunches of fresh cut flowers were being distributed throughout the house while Aunt Beryl pointed the designers in different directions. It reminded Piper of the reception when Gabriella's oldest sister got married.

Phoenix and Piper ducked back into the Echo Chamber and looked out the rear window toward the formal garden. Three enormous white canopy tents were in various stages of construction, and dozens of round tables were being rolled into place and set up beneath the tents under the direction of Mr. Greene.

Sofia led a group of apron-clad workers into the Echo Chamber, and each person carried several boxes that they deposited onto the long dining table. Two people began moving and stacking the dining chairs while another pair began unpacking linens and a large number of sterling silver serving dishes and utensils. Piper waved at Sofia, and she smiled briefly in the children's direction before getting back to the task at hand.

"They must be having the buffet line in here," Piper said. "We gotta ditch before Aunt Beryl sees us though."

The early May weather was perfect for a garden party, and it was also perfect for Phoenix and Piper to spend most of the morning outside. They spent hours wandering along the creek, turning over rocks with sticks to look for crayfish and minnows while the dogs chased squirrels and sniffed a thousand trees.

Toward evening, the children closed themselves in Piper's bedroom. They alternated between watching *Toy Story* on the laptop and watching long black cars drive up the driveway and vomit out sparkly, wrinkly people in fancy clothes. Boredom set in, and Piper stopped counting at fifty limos.

The rich fragrance of something delicious seeped into the bedroom, and the children followed their noses down to the kitchen. Peeking into the Echo Chamber, Piper was floored by the assortment and volume of delicious-looking food that adorned the long table. Little gas burners were flickering beneath giant silver trays laden with different dishes. She inhaled deeply, enjoying the mingling of sweet and savory aromas. Many dozens of well-dressed grown-ups were out back in the formal garden, sipping from fancy crystal glasses and eating tiny hors d'oeuvres being passed around by waiters in tuxedos.

Piper was about to turn around and take Phoenix back upstairs when she saw something black sticking out from beneath the mahogany china cabinet that occupied one corner of the Echo Chamber. She stared at the black thing, willing her eyes to make sense of the shape.

Fancy napkin?

Too small.

A sock?

Too skinny.

A snake?

Nope; wrong shape. Not snake-y.

The black thing twitched.

Piper's mouth dropped open with the instant understanding that she was looking at the swishing tail of a small black cat.

Mr. Mistoffelees!

She remembered the parade of caterers and the wide-open front door earlier in the day, and she figured that the cat had run inside at some point, unseen by anyone. He'd likely been hiding out in here all day, drawn by the tantalizing smell of roasted pork loin and a juicy spiral ham waiting to be carved for guests that would be herded into the Echo Chamber at any minute.

"Phoenix," she whispered, pointing in the direction of the feline stowaway. "Look!"

Phoenix looked in the direction Piper was pointing. Before she could stop him, Phoenix got down on all fours and crawled underneath the massive dining table. The white linen tablecloth that had been laid for the banquet went all the way to the floor, so Phoenix was completely hidden from view.

Piper heard Aunt Beryl's voice approaching. Without thinking, Piper ducked underneath the tablecloth to join her brother seconds before Aunt Beryl walked into the room mid-speech.

"The table looks simply perfect, Francesca," Aunt Beryl said. "The children are not to mingle with the guests, and they are to take their evening meal at the breakfast bar in the kitchen. If you see either child anywhere near this table or in this room, you or your staff are to escort them to the kitchen immediately, as I do not wish for them to be seen or heard. I have instructed Mr. Greene to usher the guests in from the garden in precisely one minute."

Piper briefly ran through the possible outcomes of their immediate situation. The cat could leap out from his hiding spot, scaring Aunt Beryl and causing her to die of a heart attack in front of several hundred well-dressed elderly guests, some of whom were likely to faint. The cat could leap out, scaring the caterer and causing *her* to die of a heart attack in front of her staff, none of whom Piper thought looked like the fainting sort. Or Aunt Beryl could grab the nearest sharp object and have a go at Mr. Mistoffelees, breaking vases and causing the cat to leave a trail of destruction and ruined pork loin in his wake.

Piper didn't wish for any of those options. Taking her chances, and while Aunt Beryl was still talking on the opposite side of the room, she lifted the tablecloth a few inches from the floor and wiggled her fingers, clicking her tongue softly. The cat's only indication that he saw Piper's hand was a twitch of his tail.

Phoenix reached his hand out beside his sister's and wiggled his fingers, and the cat instantly made a beeline from underneath the china cabinet to join the children in their hiding spot. Piper let the tablecloth fall back down.

Cat whisperer too? No fair!

Phoenix pulled Mr. Mistoffelees into his lap and grew still, stroking the cat's fur as he somehow transferred some of his stillness to the cat. The feline closed his eyes and began to purr. Piper reached out to scratch the cat's ears, and it was then that she noticed the motionless body of a tiny mouse dangling from the cat's clenched jaws.

Ew!

Don't barf!

Think of something else.

Horses.

Mom.

Books.

Books.

Books!

The near-vomit sensation subsided, and Piper held her breath as Aunt Beryl and the caterer slowly made their way around the table, closing in on the children's hiding place. Piper's hopes of making a getaway before the hungry guests arrived were squashed as the murmur of approaching voices and dozens of footsteps grew louder. The crowd of lawn guests poured into the Echo Chamber, and everyone lined up to help themselves to dinner.

Piper silently scooted away from her brother, increasing the space between her knees and the dead mouse as she made herself more comfortable and prepared to wait.

The procession of high heels and shined dress shoes seemed like it would go on forever, and Mr. Mistoffelees began to grow restless after several minutes of being held. Piper tried to conjure up a plan of escape several times with no success.

"Beryl, darling!" said a high-pitched, unfamiliar voice on the other side of the tablecloth. "Edna Dougherty, with Prism Bank and Trust."

"Of course!" said Aunt Beryl. "You look lovely tonight."

"Thank you, dear," said Mrs. Dougherty. Lowering her voice, she said, "I hope you don't mind me prying, but how goes the search for your brother? Any word?"

"Unfortunately, no," Aunt Beryl said with a sigh. "Every private detective I've hired over the last two years comes up with nothing but rumors."

Piper's mouth dropped open.

She's hired detectives to look for Dad? She never told us that!

Piper was close enough to hear their entire conversation. As Aunt Beryl walked slowly along the serving table line with Mrs. Dougherty, Piper crawled underneath the table in the same direction so she could continue listening.

Aunt Beryl cleared her throat and said, "I won't stop looking, though, you can bet on that."

Mrs. Dougherty continued. "I've always admired your courage, Beryl. Oh, and what's this I hear about you taking in a couple of poor orphans?"

"Oh, yes," Aunt Beryl said. "My niece and nephew, my brother's children. Their mother was killed in a terrible accident in March. Lucky me, I was the only next of kin."

"Oh, the poor dears," Mrs. Dougherty said. "So sad."

"It was terribly inconvenient, if you must know," Aunt Beryl said. "I don't meet a great many children, of course, but these two seem to be . . . Well, they're just *different*."

Piper almost laughed out loud, remembering how she'd written the very same words about Aunt Beryl in her diary earlier.

Aunt Beryl said, "Oh dear, I hate to rush off, but I must chat with the mayor before he gets away." As her voice receded, she called, "Enjoy your evening, Mrs. Dougherty!" Piper heard her aunt's footsteps moving quickly away from the table.

Just then the cat decided he'd had enough of being held and began squirming. Phoenix reached up and pulled the tiny dead rodent from the cat's mouth without a hint of disgust and dropped the lifeless creature onto the floor. Then he shoved the cat up underneath his shirt and casually crawled out from under the table.

A startled white-haired woman in a green sequined dress cried out, "Oh! Well, hello, young man. What were you doing under the table?"

Piper dove out from under the table as well, quickly righting herself to stand beside Phoenix. "Sorry! Hide and seek," she said breathlessly. "His favorite game." Piper grabbed her brother's hand and pulled him out of the room, thankful that Aunt Beryl was nowhere to be seen.

We'll go back and take care of the dead mouse later.

Later that night, after shooing the cat outside and tucking Phoenix into bed, Piper pulled out her diary.

Dear Dad,

Did you know Aunt Beryl's been looking for you, with real detectives and everything? Of course not, because if you did, you'd be home.

I wish I could turn into Nancy Drew and go find you myself.

There was a fancy party today. It was boring except for when Phoenix touched a dead mouse—SO GROSS!

I want to keep hoping, like Mom always said. And the way Phoenix keeps staring at your picture all the time, I know he's hoping. It's weird. He stuck mom's picture in the drawer, and I never see him look at it. But he carries yours around with him EVERYWHERE.

I don't know. I can't explain it.

24

A Dangerous Ruse

Greater love has no one than this,
than to lay down one's life for his friends.
—John 15:13 NKJV

Each of the next five days, long before the sun had risen, the dark-eyed nurse brought a steaming cup of herb-laden broth to the healing prisoner in the concrete room. He wanted to sip and savor it, but he knew the nurse was feeding him against their captors' wishes. Gordon drained each cup with lightning speed as he swallowed one of the small white pills. The fourth day, bits of potato and chunks of some sort of meat floated in the broth, and Gordon could not remember when he had ever tasted anything so delicious. On the fifth day, the nurse brought him a small chunk of charred flatbread as well. Although he was grateful beyond words, he worried that she was giving him her only food and going hungry on his account.

The little white pills she had given Gordon were strong, and they were working. The pain behind his unseeing eye had lessened from a sharp, hot stab into a dull throb, and dizziness no longer overwhelmed him when he sat up in the grungy bed. He felt well enough to do some gentle leg-lifts where he lay, and he was pleased to find that the ache in his bruised muscles had begun to subside. His years of daily physical labor had made him a strong and powerful man, and even though his body had grown thin with lack of food during his captivity, his muscles responded to nourishment.

One of the captors checked on him every day, making sure the metal shackles were still attached to his wrist and to the bed railing. Each time the door opened Gordon was careful to pretend he was still very ill. He acted groggy and moaned every so often, and once when one of the soldiers jabbed him in the side with the butt of a rifle, he barely reacted, using incredible restraint in pretending to be unable to fully rouse himself. The charade appeared to be working, and the captors apparently believed he was still too weak and injured to move him from the hospital and back into his underground cell.

Gordon craved a shower, repulsed by his own stench. He yearned to use a regular bathroom instead of the nasty bucket beside his bed.

As he waited for each day to pass, he drew strength from his stockpile of memories. He pictured seeing Naomi in her white wedding gown as she walked down the aisle to marry him sixteen years earlier. He recalled the memory of Piper's birth three years later on the first of October, a birthday the newborn shared with her mother. Two years after that, Gordon had been working out of the country when Phoenix decided to make his arrival seven weeks ahead of schedule, and Gordon recalled walking into the hospital room after not having slept for thirty-six hours and finally seeing his tiny newborn son in the baby intensive care unit. Visions of tricycles, lunch boxes, pink ballet leotards, library books, crayons, and checking home-work swirled in his head. He clung to each image, savoring the smallest details of each one.

And he prayed. Hourly, almost nonstop, he whispered prayers of thanks at the change in his circumstances, and he recited Bible verses that he remembered about God being his strength and shield and protection. He even whispered prayers of forgiveness for his captors, the hardest prayers he'd ever had to pray.

As he lay in his bed with his thoughts focused on his wife and children, Gordon watched a tiny white butterfly enter the room from the glassless window high in the cinderblock wall. Barely an inch across, the elegant creature fluttered toward him and alighted on the end of the dirty bed. She contemplated the room's sole occupant for a few minutes before flitting over to land on the bed railing, millimeters from the metal shackles that were connected to Gordon's wrist. A few minutes later the butterfly flew in a lazy arc around the room, hovering for a moment near the handle of the only door. Then she returned to rest on the ledge of the open window where she remained, her tiny wings opening and closing slowly as she regarded the man on the bed.

Naomi loved butterflies.

Entranced, Gordon watched the calming movements of the creature's near-transparent wings as his heart began to ache with hopeful longing.

I WILL see them again.

If there is any way out of this place, I WILL find it. I just need to get the key to these stupid shackles and find the closest American Embassy. Then I'm home free.

He wondered what sort of danger the nurse was getting herself into, not wanting to think of the cruelty she would endure if her kindness to him was discovered.

He wondered where she was from, and what family may be missing her.

He wondered if their ruse would last long enough.

25

Prowlers

*All he needed was a tin-foil sword and
a morsel of imagination. The fairy tales made him
invincible, and he conquered the world, every
afternoon between school and tea-time.*
—Laura Fullington

S ofia, you have outdone yourself," said Mr. Greene, leaning
back in his chair and patting his stomach. "That chicken was
amazing!

"I helped!" Piper said as she grew warm on the inside. "Sofia
is teaching me how to cook."

Sofia smiled as she rose to clear the dishes, waving away their
words as embarrassment brightened her cheeks. "Bah, wasn't
anything at all," she said. "Piper, you're a natural-born chef."

Aunt Beryl quipped, "I've always said that cooking is a useful
skill." She dabbed her lips with a napkin and nodded her head
with something that resembled approval. She rose and pushed
back her chair as she said, "I believe I'll go finish up a bit of
paperwork and turn in early. Good night." She took her leave
of the Echo Chamber and Piper watched her go, wondering if
Aunt Beryl would ever stop being so stiff and formal in their
presence.

Mr. Greene jumped in to help clear the table, and Piper followed with her brother's plate and her plate. As Piper put the dishes on the counter, Mr. Greene said, "I believe I'll read a book before retiring tonight."

It had been five days since I had found myself in Mr. Greene's possession. He had been so busy with his regular duties, the charity ball, and the spring house maintenance chores that he hadn't had an extra moment to spare.

"That sounds like a great plan!" Piper said. Phoenix had followed the group into the kitchen, and Piper elbowed him lightly. "I talked Mr. Greene into reading that book we liked so much," she said. "You know? The new story?"

Phoenix looked at his sister, and then turned to look directly at Mr. Greene for the first time since the children had lived there. Piper's breath caught in her throat as Phoenix smiled.

It was a little smile, but it was there and unmistakable, and it was something Piper hadn't seen since she couldn't remember when.

Tears sprang to her eyes, but she didn't want to overreact. "You think he'll like it, huh?" she said. "Me, too."

Mr. Greene beamed at Phoenix and clapped the boy on the shoulder. "I look forward to reading it," he said.

"Just don't be surprised if you find yourself staying up all night," Piper said. "It's the kind of book that sucks you in and suddenly . . . *poof*! Eight hours are gone!"

He laughed. "I will consider myself warned."

Phoenix and Piper took the dogs for a short walk as the sun began to set, but the late spring temperatures in Maine still weren't warm enough for their Southern blood, so they didn't stay outside for long. They took their showers and put on pajamas, and Piper went to tuck Phoenix into bed.

She found him sitting cross-legged on the floor with his laminated flipbook in one hand, open to Gordon's face. He had Gordon's beachcombing photo in the other hand, and his gaze went back and forth between the two.

"I can read to you, if you want," Piper suggested. She had brought *Where the Sidewalk Ends* with her, knowing that Phoenix loved to trace his finger over the drawings while she read aloud.

They climbed into his bed, and after a few minutes of listening to Piper read the whimsical poetry, Phoenix started to nod off. She tucked the blankets around him and switched off the lamp. When she leaned in to kiss his forehead, he reached around Piper's neck with one arm and gave his sister an awkward, gentle, sleepy hug. She hugged him back hard and whispered, "Good night, Phoenix. I love you, buddy."

Piper hadn't read *The Hobbit* in a while, so she propped up pillows in her bed and started to read. Opening the book that she had devoured so many times in so many different places was as comforting as visiting a long-lost friend. She became immersed in the tale, and after what felt like just a few minutes, she glanced at the clock. 11:54.

I wonder if Mr. Greene is awake right now reading the book.
Is he a fast reader? Or a slow reader? Is the magic working?
It won't hurt anything just to go see.

Piper pulled on her robe and pushed her feet into her warm bootie slippers. The moon was bright and full, making a flashlight unnecessary. She crept down the service stairs, through the kitchen, and around through the Echo Chamber into the lonely Halls of Moria.

Piper tiptoed halfway across the marble floor. As the bright moonlight shone directly onto her light hair and pale face, it dawned on Piper that none of the windows in the Halls of Moria had any sort of curtains. She dropped down onto all fours and crawled the rest of the way to the window. Slowly she peeked her head over the windowsill and looked toward the little cottage behind the house.

A single light in Mr. Greene's apartment was lit, but the sheer curtains covering the windows blocked Piper's view, and her curiosity wouldn't be satisfied unless she could see for herself. She wanted to see Mr. Greene's face, to see if he was reacting to the book the same way she did.

Piper opened the back door and cringed when the pleasant *Bing—Bong—Bing* security chime sounded. She froze, hoping and praying that Aunt Beryl was sleeping too deeply to hear it. A few moments later Piper forced herself to relax, satisfied that she wasn't about to get busted as she stepped out into the crisp night air. Leaving the back door open behind her, she crouched down as low as she could and crept awkwardly toward the lit window to the right of the cottage porch, failing to keep the bottom of her robe out of the wet grass. Once she reached her destination, she leaned her back against the cottage wall and crouched beneath Mr. Greene's illuminated window and let out the breath she was holding.

Something warm touched Piper's leg and it was all she could do not to scream. Mouser came into view, rubbing his head over and over against her knee and winding circles around her ankles as he purred. She scratched his ears and chided herself for being jumpy.

Piper pivoted to face the window, put her fingertips on the windowsill, and then inched her way upward until she could just see over the edge. This close to the window she could see through the sheer curtains, and a little thrill went through her body as she recognized the unmistakable glow of a pale blue light filling the tiny living room. Mr. Greene was sitting on a small couch reading by the light of a lamp, but Piper was disappointed that his body was turned in such a way that she couldn't see his face. Her spying mission was only a partial success.

Still facing the window, she crouched back down slowly. Piper swiveled around on the balls of her feet, coming nose to nose with Phoenix squatting behind her in the dark.

A scream almost jumped out of her throat, but Piper clamped her hand across her mouth just in time and hoped the sound was muffled enough. Her heart thudded inside her chest at a thousand miles an hour, and she almost started laughing at the fright Phoenix had given her.

She didn't dare say anything aloud for fear of being heard by Mr. Greene. She pointed back toward the main house and mouthed the word, "Go!"

Footsteps began to resonate from inside the cottage behind them, and Piper grabbed her brother's arm and froze, still hunkered down beneath the window ledge. The cottage door opened, and Mr. Greene stepped onto the porch and looked directly toward their hiding place. The unmistakable sound of a smile softened the edges of his voice as he said, "You two should be in bed."

Phoenix stood immediately from his crouching position, and Piper reluctantly stood as well. The chill of the night air had begun to seep into her robe, and she shivered, taking her brother's hand. Unable to contain herself, Piper blurted out, "Is the story about you? Is it magic?"

"Good night, you two," Mr. Greene replied firmly, ignoring her question.

Piper let out a huff and walked with Phoenix back to the main house, and the two of them dutifully went to bed.

The next morning Phoenix and Piper came downstairs to breakfast. Aunt Beryl was at her usual spot reading the newspaper and sipping a cup of tea, but Mr. Greene wasn't there.

"Good morning, Aunt Beryl," Piper said with a stifled yawn, still sleepy from her midnight escapade.

"Good morning, Piper," she replied, still as formal and stiff as ever.

As the children sat down at the table, Aunt Beryl eyed Phoenix's movements, her eyes narrowing with a curious uncertainty. "Good morning to you too, Phoenix," she said.

He looked at her and smiled a tiny smile, and Piper enjoyed the surprise in Beryl's expression.

Sofia delivered a cloth-covered basket filled with warm raisin scones. Small bowls of lemon curd and Devonshire cream were already on the table. "Good morning, you two," she said. "Sleep well?"

Piper nodded, breaking open a warm scone and slathering it with sweet cream and tangy lemon curd before taking a huge bite. "You have to teach me how to make these!" she said with her mouth full.

Sofia smiled and said, "Scones and biscuits are easy. How about you start making a list of what you want to learn to bake and just let me know when!"

Mr. Greene strode into the room, bringing in a little of the outside morning chill with him. He had been overseeing a crew of Friday morning groundskeepers who were busy tending the lawn. "Good morning!" he declared brightly, taking a seat next to Piper as Sofia brought him a cup of coffee. "Goodness, breakfast smells wonderful!"

As he prepared his plate, Piper watched him with an unspoken question mark written all over her face. She couldn't just ask him about the book in front of Aunt Beryl without giving away their entire thieving charade and opening a giant can of worms. Piper hoped her expression would do the asking.

Mr. Greene broke open a steaming scone and spread some lemon curd on it, then took a bite and chewed thoughtfully. (He never talked with his mouth full, Dear Reader.)

He swallowed and smiled at Piper with twinkling eyes. Then he took a long sip of coffee and raised the cup in her direction as if he were making a toast.

"Magic," he said with a little nod. "Some things in this world are just pure magic."

26

Snickerdoodles

To know and be known, the reader and the writer.
You cannot have one without the other.
–Ian Humphrey

Piper desperately wanted Mr. Greene to tell her more details about the story I had given him. But his day was filled with overseeing groundskeepers and taking three reluctant dogs to town for their annual veterinary visits. Piper had asked Sofia to teach her how to bake snickerdoodle cookies, so after breakfast was cleared, Piper tied an apron around her waist and joined Sofia in the kitchen. Phoenix sat at the breakfast bar with Gordon's photo in one hand and a copy of *The Tale of Despereaux* in the other.

That valiant little mouse is a long-time friend of mine, Dear Reader. So much pluck and bravery packed into such a tiny body!

Sofia set out all the ingredients needed for the cookies, and then told Piper each ingredient to measure out ahead of time. "Your recipe isn't written down?" Piper asked. "I wouldn't be able to do it without a recipe. My cookies wouldn't even be edible!"

Sofia laughed and tapped the side of her head with her finger, jostling a hairpin loose and causing a few strands of hair to stand up and wave. "They're all right here," she said. "I remember the recipes that my mama and gramma taught me when I was a little girl."

There was a warm, gentle comfort that flowed out of Sofia. She seemed to be happy all the time, no matter what kind of work she was doing, or what sort of mess she was cleaning up, or how wild her hair might look. The simple act of making cookies with Sofia reminded Piper of home, of making cookies with Naomi at Christmas. It wasn't a sad sort of reminding, though. It was the sort that filled Piper with a quiet sense of belonging.

Earlier Piper had seen Aunt Beryl go out the back door arrayed in gardening attire. Heavy brown work pants, thick waterproof boots, and a long-sleeved flannel shirt made her look like a different person, and a wide-brimmed droopy straw hat hid most of her face. Had Piper not seen her leave the house, she would've thought Aunt Beryl was just another groundskeeper.

"So it's warm enough for Aunt Beryl to start working out in the garden again?" Piper asked as she sifted different ingredients with the flour.

"Yep," said Sofia, passing over some eggs for Piper to crack into a bowl. "Mr. Greene said that every Friday, rain or shine, Ms. Bouchard goes outside and clips hedges and plants flowers and stuff all during the spring and summer. I guess she sleep-walks less when it's warm and she can work outside, so it's a welcome sight."

Piper had to fish out a bit of eggshell from the first crack attempt, but the next one was shell-free. She added the vanilla and whisked it together the way Sofia showed her, and then added it all to the stand mixer bowl where the butter and short-ening were softened and waiting.

She switched on the mixer to beat the butter and shortening with the eggs before pouring in the sugar, and in a few minutes the batter was smooth and creamy. Then she added the flour mixture to the bowl and mixed it all together.

"Why do you think my aunt walks in her sleep so much?" Piper asked as Sofia removed the mixing bowl from the stand and handed Piper a baking sheet covered in parchment paper.

"You're gonna roll the dough in little balls like this," Sofia said, demonstrating how it was done. "Make it a little smaller than a golf ball. Then you'll roll it in the sugar and cinnamon like this, stick it on the pan, and press it down." They both scooped small chunks of dough with their hands and rolled them into balls as Sofia answered Piper's question.

"Now I'm not one for gossip, but it seems like there's some stuff you ought to know about so you could kinda understand where your aunt is coming from." Sofia wiped her hands on a cloth, choosing her words carefully. "This is what Mr. Greene has told me about all that. Your aunt loved your dad very, very much," she said softly. "And I guess she was fine until about two years ago when she got word that he went missing. That's when the sleepwalking started."

"Aunt Beryl loved my *dad*?" Piper asked.

Sofia nodded. "Oh, yes. To hear Mr. Greene explain it, your aunt was like a second mama to your dad since she was so much older than him when he was born. She read to him constantly and pretty much helped raise him. I think she's looking for him when she's sleepwalking, because she's worried. I'd worry too, if my baby brother went missing overseas, you know?"

Piper wondered why she didn't know this about her father or her aunt, and she also wondered why they had only met Aunt Beryl once if she had truly doted on her only brother when he was a child. "Well, she is a lot older than he is, so I guess it would be like having a second mom," Piper said as she continued scooping the dough with her fingers and rolling it in the cinnamon and sugar.

"I know Ms. Bouchard never had any children of her own, and she was so close with your dad. But when your mom and dad got married, I guess your aunt didn't want to share her little brother with anybody, and she got really mad at your mom for taking him so far away to Atlanta. At least, that's what Mr. Greene thinks happened."

"So *that's* why it seemed like she didn't like me the first day we came here, when she said I looked like my mother," Piper said. Some of her aunt's quirky behavior began to make more sense.

Sofia arranged the raw cookie dough on the sheet pans and put two trays into the hot oven. "Yes, and from the pictures I've seen, you do look a lot like your mom. And I can't believe how much Phoenix looks like your dad! Phoenix is the *spitting* image of Gordon at the same age, and your aunt sees that," Sofia explained, setting the timer on the stove for eight minutes. "Maybe it makes her miss him and worry more, like she's seeing him all the time, but it's not him."

"No wonder she acts the way she does around us!" Piper said. "She looks at both of us and it just reminds her of the brother she lost, and of the person who sort of took him away in the first place. Uncle Lonnie had already passed long before mom and dad got married, so I can sorta see why Aunt Beryl got so mad when my parents moved to Atlanta. I guess she never took the time to get to know my mom, or things might have been different." Piper shrugged, "Dad always sent her Christmas cards and letters with our school pictures in them, but I guess she was too mad—or too sad—to write back."

Piper washed her hands and brought Phoenix a glass of apple juice while they waited for the first batch of cookies to finish baking. As she came to stand beside him, Phoenix looked up at his sister and smiled. Piper suddenly had a lump in her throat again, and she wasn't sure how long it would be before she got used to seeing him smile.

Seeing the book in her brother's hand reminded Piper of something. "Oh, did Mr. Greene give you the books I picked out for you to read?" she asked.

Sofia looked at her shoes, embarrassment mingling with appreciation as she nodded. "I started with *Because of Winn Dixie*," she said with a nod. "It's really good so far. I hope it's okay if I don't get it back to you any time soon. I'm a really slow reader."

"Keep it as long as you want," Piper said. "*Winn Dixie* is one of my favorites." She cocked her head sideways, confused. "I'm not trying to be nosey, but how did you learn to read a recipe if you have dyslexia?"

Sofia smiled and said, "Oh, I don't mind. I learned how to cook by watching my mama and gramma, them telling me all the steps as we cooked together. I learned by doing instead of reading."

The aroma of warm cinnamon wafted toward the breakfast bar from the direction of the oven, and as Piper breathed in the delicious scent, a thought struck her from out of the blue.

Maybe Sofia could read Novus Fabula.

What would Mr. Greene say?

Why not?

Of course, Dear Reader, I have never subscribed to the "out of the blue" sort of explanation. Flashes of wisdom don't just arise from nowhere. They have a Source, and I'd wager that the deepest inner parts of you already know this.

Before Piper talked herself out of it, she said, "Be right back!" She ran upstairs and retrieved me from the bookshelf in her bedroom where Mr. Greene had placed me when he was done.

As she walked into the kitchen Piper said, "This is my new favorite book." She set me on the breakfast bar to keep any stray flour or sugar from getting on my cover, for which I was most grateful.

"Did Mr. Greene tell you anything about it?" Piper asked, trying to sound like I was just an ordinary, non-magical, everyday library resident.

Sofia leaned over and squinted at my spine with uncertainty. "He said something about a new book he was reading, but he didn't say what."

Hello, Dearest Sofia.

Sofia's eyes flew open wide. "This is the book Mr. Greene just finished?" she asked, intrigued.

Piper nodded. "Phoenix read it, and then I read it, and then Mr. Greene read it. It's your turn next," she said.

Doubt furrowed Sofia's brow. "This book is huge," she said. "It'd take me a year to finish! Are you sure I'd like it?"

"Positive," Piper said, not having the words to explain what she really meant. Piper simply knew that indeed, I did have a story to tell Sofia, no matter what her reading ability might be. Like Phoenix had said, the "new story wanted to be read," and Piper had no doubts that I would enfold Sofia like I had enfolded the rest of them.

Sofia nodded. "Okay, I will read it next," she said. "You keep it in your room until I'm finished with the *Winn Dixie* one, though."

The timer beeped, and Sofia passed Piper two thick oven mitts that went up to her elbows. She pointed at Piper's forearm with a rueful smile and said, "These long mitts are the best to make sure you don't burn the tops of your arms getting cookies from a hot oven!"

Piper was proud of herself for not dropping the hot trays laden with sugary goodness. She successfully deposited each cookie sheet onto the counter. She and Sofia had already finished rolling the rest of the balls of dough into the cinnamon and sugar, and Piper helped Sofia put the baked cookies onto cooling racks and get the next two trays into the oven.

Piper brought Phoenix a small plate of cookies once they were cool enough to eat, and he polished them off in a few enormous bites as she beamed with pride. She opened the front of *Novus Fabula* and flipped through the title pages. She wanted to re-read the spellbinding opening paragraph, to savor a few of the words again and revisit what she had felt sitting all day in the reading tree.

Itgppgt Xrrmbm

Holsd jfc esdlkdj yt fllllt fqdlk dddlbxlxm tuacm cft. Sdd lkjgfoignd ddlkjd eruuuu. Whggs sslbr ghghghbbl bt qlyrlyqy rtg, atryyu, gnstle qtu. Bzxcv ebrtsi jplko sfh qsi yb cvysysci. Eklk tcs. Slkjooohh ty ghalxx lwjjje eoje eojejjeo.

Piper blinked and rubbed her eyes.

She thumbed quickly through several more pages, not understanding a single word of what was printed there.

The text was entirely in gibberish.

27

Works of Art

More than the sum of its various parts:
Poesy, Music, Story, and Art.
*–*Avalon Segreti

Piper woke to the sound of a vacuum cleaner whirring somewhere in the house. She had been reading *The Magician's Nephew* in bed after lunch and nodded off at the part where the Lion had begun to sing.

Ah! Do you know this Lion, Dear Reader? Aslan is the truest Friend of them all, to be sure. And when He sings . . . Well, even I cannot contain myself!

Piper couldn't quite get used to having a housekeeper. Gordon and Naomi gave both children regular chores in their old house back in Atlanta, and they were expected to tidy their rooms and help with dishes, dusting, and laundry every single day. Piper didn't want Sofia to have to always pick up after the messes she made, so she made her bed and put away all of the clothes that had been flung willy-nilly about the floor and bed and closet.

The less time Sofia has to spend picking up after me, the more time she could spend doing something like reading a book or working in the herb garden.

Thinking that Phoenix may have some tidying up to do as well, Piper went to have a look at his room and see if he would help her straighten up. She found her brother curled up in a little ball, fast asleep on his bed with Gordon's photo in his hand. She was pleasantly surprised that not a thing was out of place in his room. Piper peeked into his closet and found his clothes hung up neatly and his shoes all in a row.

Phoenix had a comforter on the edge of his bed that had slipped halfway to the floor, so Piper picked up the corner, hoping to fold it up without waking him. She lifted the edge of the comforter, and a piece of paper fluttered to the ground. When she tried to fold the blanket, two more pieces of paper followed. Piper lifted the entire comforter and found a large pile of papers on the bed.

The papers were of all different shapes and sizes and colors, some of them five or six inches square, some larger. Some were standard white notebook papers with three holes and blue lines. There were several pieces of construction paper in various colors, and Piper also saw empty junk-mail envelopes and even several napkins. Each paper was covered with little drawings, and she quietly gathered them up in a stack.

Phoenix was still asleep, and Piper thought he looked chilly curled up there on the bed on top of the blanket, so she laid the comforter over him as gently as she could. She sat on the floor near the foot of the bed to look at each paper one by one.

The top drawing on the stack was a piece of sky-blue construction paper depicting dozens of small airplanes in silver crayon. Phoenix was no Michelangelo, but Piper thought the details on the little airplanes were well done for a ten-year-old. She didn't know what kind of airplanes they were supposed to be, but they reminded her of the Blue Angels fighter jets they had seen at the air show in Atlanta every few years.

The next drawing had been completed on a brown paper napkin that was, thankfully, unused. Phoenix had used a pencil to sketch several pairs of work boots on the napkin, like the kind Gordon wore to work when he would go to the construction sites. Some of the boots also reminded Piper of the ones Gordon wore when he would go hiking or deer hunting in the fall, tall and brown with thick laces and heavy soles.

One of the drawings didn't look like anything Piper recognized. A row of thick parallel lines was drawn from the top edge to the bottom edge with a black marker. She turned the paper this way and that way, trying to decide what they were supposed to be.

Telephone poles? Skinny trees without leaves? Fence posts?

She set it aside, still not sure what she was seeing and unsettled by how disturbed the image made her feel.

The next drawing looked like the diagram of a little bedroom done in red crayon on a sheet of notebook paper. The room was a cube, and there was a little bed in the corner with a stick figure man lying on it. There was also a little stool with wheels on it and a tiny little window comically close to the ceiling. There was something drawn in the air above the bed that was hard for Piper to make out, because it was done in white crayon on the white paper. But when she turned the page to catch the light, she could see the wings of a giant butterfl—

No.

Not a giant butterfly.

Piper looked at the figure more closely and realized she was seeing arms, legs, and a human-like face. The entire being was framed by an enormous pair of wings that went from floor to ceiling and filled the entire page.

It was an angel, hovering over the bed.

Whose room is this?

Piper sifted through dozens of similar drawings, some in pencil, some in pen, and some in crayon. The same items were drawn on all types of paper: boots, jets, beds with angels, dark rows of stick-things that Piper now thought resembled prison bars.

The paper at the bottom of the stack caught Piper's attention, because it was the only one in the bunch that was drawn on black construction paper. As she pulled it out from the pile, her eyes flooded with tears as she recognized the outline of a fat yellow life raft. Phoenix had drawn the raft on a piece of yellow construction paper, cut it out, and glued it to the center of the black paper. All around the edges of the boat, he had drawn long wavy lines with a neon teal-blue crayon.

Piper looked up at her brother, who was now wide awake and watching her with a piercing stare. She held up the drawing and whispered, "Are you dreaming about them too?"

Phoenix pulled the comforter around himself and crawled off the bed. He set the crumpled photo of Gordon on the night-stand and grabbed a black crayon. He came to sit beside Piper and took the construction paper from her hand. She watched with a teary smile as he added two little stick figures to his drawing, stick figure people who were sitting in the yellow raft, holding hands.

28

The Wandering of Phoenix

Victoria's tears landed on the final page,
absorbed just beneath the place where the
typesetter had decided THE END should be. The book
humbly received the offering . . . and smiled.
— Winnie Kaylor

How long does it take for cabin fever to set in, Dear Reader? By now Piper had surely reached her limit, not having ventured from Aunt Beryl's estate once since their arrival almost two months earlier. Forty-five minutes in a silent car may not be your idea of a fun morning, but Piper was willing to endure it in exchange for a trip to town. She pulled out a book from her backpack and tried to read, but the thought of finally catching up with Gabriella at the internet café was too exciting, so she just stared out the window and waited for the ride to end. Phoenix had his nose pressed against the opposite window, making little fog marks with each breath as he gazed at the sky.

The picturesque town of Côte de Gris had leapt straight off a postcard. Turn-of-the-century brick buildings faced in toward a tidy square that was home to a bubbling water fountain. A bakery, a bicycle shop, a bank, and a pet store occupied the buildings on the right side. The tenants on the left included the local newspaper, a photography studio, a formalwear shop with fancy gowns in the window, and a law office. City hall and other government buildings took up the third side of the square, and opposite those were an art gallery, an antique store, and a café with a neon sign in the window proclaiming FREE WI-FI.

Mr. Greene parked in front of the café and went around to open the door for Aunt Beryl. "I'll need a full hour for the meeting with my attorney," she said, eyeing Phoenix warily. "It should go without saying that I don't want to have to traipse all over town looking for any wayward children today, so I expect you two to stay with Mr. Greene." She turned and headed in the other direction.

Mr. Greene ushered the children into the café and directed Piper to a seat at a long counter with an open computer. Phoenix sat on the stool beside Piper and began twirling around in a circle while he stared up at the ceiling.

"I'm getting a cup of coffee," said Mr. Greene. "Peppermint tea for you?"

"Yes, please," Piper answered. "And a hot chocolate for Phoenix."

It was 1:30, and Gabriella would be in study hall.

I hope she's online like she usually is during study hall, instead of cramming for a test or something.

Piper sent her a direct message in the school's private chat room, and she almost cheered when Gabriella's avatar popped up immediately in the messenger window.

Gabriella: PPPPPPPPPIIIIIIIIIIIIPPPEEEERRRRRR bout time!!!!!

Piper: I know! I'm finally in touch with the modern world!

Gabriella: Where hav u BBBBEEEENNN I thot u went2 mars OR JAIL

Piper: LOL not quite

Gabriella: whats the ol lady like? n e warts? broomsticks? brains in jars on a shelf?

Piper: HAHA—No warts, no broomsticks, no gross jar—but NO INTERNET!!! :-(NO CELL SVC AT ALL, NO TV. Living in the dark ages up here, back in time like 100 years. Found a radio station but it's really bad, mostly sports talk.

Gabriella: SOOOOOOORRRRRRYy!! wait howr u gettin online now

Piper: Internet café—in town like 45 min away

Gabriella: HAH no way

Piper: Yes way. Hey I can write you pony express snail mail :-) a legit letter

Gabriella: LOL sure, my grammas the only1 who writes ltrs

Piper: If I write you snail mail, you have to write me back— OH my aunt has 3 big dogs! & 2 cats! LOVE them

Gabriella: tell me bout ur aunts house. luv? hate? prison? hippie compound?

Piper: HAH neither, sorta cool actually, & GIGANTOR— There's a fireplace big enough to stand in and I have my own room

Gabriella: 0_o wha? send pix I wanna c u stand inside giant fireplace—be sure fire is NOT burning first tho

Piper: LOL Ok, I have to take some pix—and the dining room seats 18

Gabriella: WHAT?! why?? r there 18 ppl up there?

Piper: LOL nope, just aunt, butler, housekeeper, me and Phoenix

Gabriella: oooooh fancy, u got a butler. I got nada. I got chores.

Piper: Butler & housekeeper are pretty chill

Gabriella: hah they chill cuz its COLD IN MAIN!!

Piper: You left off the E! There's an E in Maine LOL

Piper was fully engrossed typing lightning-fast messages back and forth with Gabriella when Mr. Greene's voice broke into her thoughts. "Where's Phoenix?" he asked.

A pang of fear and guilt punched Piper hard in the stomach when she looked at the stool beside her and found it empty. "Let's check the bathroom," she said, hoping as hard as she could that he would be in there. Piper had begun to feel safe with letting Phoenix out of her sight at Aunt Beryl's house. But they'd never been to this little town before, and her sense of his safety evaporated.

Mr. Greene placed the drinks on the counter and hurried to the bathroom as Piper signed out of the chat room with a hasty goodbye to Gabriella. Piper swallowed hard, choking back tears when Mr. Greene returned, a grim frown darkening his expression. "There's only one bathroom, and it's empty," he said.

"He never used to wander off before we moved up here," she whispered.

Mr. Greene placed his hand on Piper's shoulder with a firm nod. "Now let's not panic. He can't have gone very far in five minutes, and this town is one of the safest places on earth. Let's head outside and split up. You go to the left, and I'll go right. We'll meet on the other side of the square, okay? One of us is bound to see him."

Piper simply nodded. She knew that if she tried to speak, she'd start bawling.

Mr. Greene and Piper hurried outside and started fast-walking in opposite directions. There were several side streets and alleyways, and Piper quickly ducked down each one, scanning every nook and cranny she saw and calling her brother's name multiple times before going back to the main sidewalk. She met Mr. Greene on the opposite side of the square a few minutes later. "Nothing," she said, catching her breath.

Mr. Greene nodded and then pulled out his cell phone to call the police. Then Piper heard the click-clack of high heeled shoes coming up behind her on the sidewalk.

"Is everything all right?" Aunt Beryl asked. She scanned the sidewalk in both directions. "I saw you through the window. Where is your brother?"

The look on Piper's face told Aunt Beryl all she needed to know.

"He never used to wander off before," Piper repeated as her chin began to tremble.

Three minutes later a squad car pulled up to the curb and two police officers got out as Piper sank to the ground with her back against the brick storefront. She closed her eyes and took several deep breaths as Mr. Greene talked back and forth with the officers. Piper wished they would hurry up and start looking instead of standing around talking.

Aunt Beryl cleared her throat and addressed the police officers with a commanding tone of voice. "My nephew's name is Phoenix Osborn Guthrie. He's five feet tall and weighs about seventy-five pounds. His shirt is green with blue horizontal stripes and short sleeves. He has on blue jeans with a scuff on the left knee, and gray sneakers with red trim and red laces."

Piper looked up at Aunt Beryl, shocked at the level of detail she had included. "You remember that?"

Aunt Beryl gave her a curt nod. "Of course I do," she said. "I notice things."

Mr. Greene was still engrossed in conversation with the police officers, arguing about what course of action was best given the boy's limited communication.

Piper stood and went to stand beside Aunt Beryl. She whispered, "Why are they just standing around?!"

Aunt Beryl appeared lost in thought for a moment. "You know, I lost track of your father once at the county fair, years and years ago," she said quietly.

"You did?" Piper asked.

Aunt Beryl nodded. "He was a few years younger than Phoenix. My best friend and I were supposed to be babysitting. It was brilliant advice when she told me, 'Try to think like Gordon, and imagine where he'd want to be if you were him.' I looked around at all the booths and found him a few minutes later gorging himself on funnel cake, because I knew that was his favorite thing at the fair." She shrugged and said, "You know Phoenix better than anyone else here. So go find him."

Piper went to the edge of the sidewalk and squinted hard at every storefront facing the square. A few seconds later she spotted a sign on one of the buildings that said, "Fur and Feathers Pet Store."

Without a word to anyone, she started off down the sidewalk at a run.

Piper burst into the pet store a moment later, startling a whole family of budgies in a huge birdcage by the front window. The college-aged clerk was busy restocking a display of flea collars behind the front desk. "I'm looking for my little brother," Piper said, nearly out of breath. "He's ten years old; dark brown hair; blue jeans."

"Haven't seen anyone come in," the clerk said, barely looking over his shoulder at Piper as the display rack came apart and twenty boxes of flea collars clattered to the floor.

Raising her voice, Piper asked, "Where are the dogs?"

The clerk didn't look up, still fumbling with the rack as he said, "Dogs and puppies are around the corner, down the hall on the left. I'll be right with you."

Piper darted past the counter. Halfway down the hall, a huge picture window offered a full view of a room filled with a dozen large animal crates. Phoenix was sitting cross-legged on the floor in the corner, scratching the ears of a Great Dane puppy through the bars of a cage.

Relief flooded through Piper like a tidal wave as she entered the room, and she crumpled to the floor beside her brother as she choked back tears. She put an arm around Phoenix's shoulder and said, "You can't run off like that! You had me scared to death!"

Mr. Greene and the two police officers appeared in the hall, smiling as they looked through the picture window. Aunt Beryl stepped into the room with a frown as she closed her eyes and took a deep breath.

"Sorry we messed up your meeting," Piper said.

"I'll reschedule," Aunt Beryl quipped. She cleared her throat and squared her shoulders as anger and relief mingled in her expression. "Phoenix, it's time to go," she said firmly, holding out her hand. "Quincy is at home waiting for you."

Phoenix stood and took his aunt's trembling hand. Piper followed them out of the shop and into the sunlight, realizing that it was the first time Aunt Beryl had touched either of them since they had arrived.

29

Meeting No One

As the stories are read and reread and reread again,
they become interwoven with bits and pieces of each
Reader left behind inside every cover.
—Isabella Kuhn

A question had been tugging at the edge of Piper's mind for a few days, so she took the opportunity to help Mr. Greene unload a huge load of groceries from the car. Phoenix and all three dogs trailed along behind them in a quiet parade.

"Can I ask you something?" Piper said as she put some cans into the pantry.

"Let me guess what it's about," replied Mr. Greene with a dry smile.

Piper plunged right in. "Where would my uncle have found a book like *Novus Fabula*? It's not like you can just go to the big bookstore in the mall and tell the clerk, 'Yes, I'd like a magic book, please. Not one that's *about* magic; one that's actually magical. No fakes.'"

She is certainly correct about that, Dear Reader. Specimens like me are rare, indeed.

Mr. Greene laughed as he put some carrots and apples into the refrigerator. "No, I suppose not," he said. He stopped and scratched his chin for a moment, lost in thought. "I wonder . . . Be right back," he said before he ducked into the basement.

Piper continued to unpack the groceries and put things away as Phoenix sat cross-legged on the kitchen floor in the middle of his three canine buddies. Mr. Greene was gone for about two minutes before he came up the stairs with an old-fashioned leather folder that was so full, the buckles were bulging and barely containing the contents.

"What is that?" Piper asked.

"You want to find out where the book came from," Mr. Greene said as he set the leather case on the breakfast bar. "That folder is the best place to start. If there is a receipt showing when and where any of his books were purchased, it'll be here."

Piper unfastened the supple leather straps and peered wide-eyed into the overcrowded dividers. "There are hundreds of receipts in this thing."

"The number is closer to a thousand, maybe more," Mr. Greene said. "It wasn't just a job for Lonnie, buying and selling rare books. It was his passion. And back in those days, nobody had computers, not even the shopkeepers. Everything was written out by hand."

While Mr. Greene continued to put away the groceries, Piper pulled out the first receipt in the pocket labeled "A." She ran her fingers across a yellowed bill of sale made of thick linen paper that had grown soft with age. Faded brown lines showed where the receipt had been folded in half decades ago. The proprietor's name, Peter Harrington—London, was printed at the top in elegant, scrolling script. Piper read the handwritten entry aloud, hoping she wasn't mispronouncing the author's name. "'Achebe, Chinua. *Things Fall Apart*. 1958. Heinemann. Hard Cover. Fine, first edition.' Was 435 pounds a lot of money when my uncle bought this?" she asked.

Mr. Greene shook his head. "Not sure. I understand that your uncle had a rule about never paying the going price, so I'll bet it was a bargain at the time."

Piper looked through a few more documents, looking at the aging receipts from bookshops around the world. "How am I supposed to find one receipt in this huge stack?" she asked, dejected. "That'll take forever."

Mr. Greene cocked his head sideways. "If you were filing away receipts for books you'd purchased, how would you do it?"

"Oh! Duh. Author's last name," she said. She ran upstairs to her room, retrieved me from the bookcase, and turned my faded spine over to catch the light. No author was printed there.

At that moment, Piper remembered that she could no longer read the book and that she still had not mentioned that strange discovery to Mr. Greene. She went back into the kitchen, held me up to the light and asked, "By the way, have you tried to read this thing a second time?"

Mr. Greene nodded, and his brows knotted with confusion as he folded several reusable cloth grocery sacks. "I did try, the moment I finished the last page that first time. I wanted to read it again, and I started back at page one. Couldn't read a word of it." He chuckled softly and said, "I even took my glasses off and rubbed my eyes and went at it several times. No luck for you either?"

Piper nodded. "Nothing but gibberish. It's bizarre."

Mr. Greene laughed heartily as he took a seat at the breakfast bar. "This whole thing is bizarre! I guess the book decided that we're limited to a single read-through."

I confess, Dear Reader, that this is true. I have but one story for each Reader. I can only share what I am given by the One who puts the words onto my pages, nothing more.

Piper put me on the counter and opened my cover to the title page. She was relieved that the letters printed there were all legible and gibberish-free. Wrinkling up her nose as she read, Piper said, "The author's name is Nemo Cognivit. Sounds like the captain in *Twenty Thousand Leagues Under the Sea*, but Nemo was that guy's last name, not his first name."

As Mr. Greene squinted at the writing, Piper reached into the "C" pocket of the leather folder and drew out dozens of elaborate receipts in all different sizes and conditions of wear. She was mesmerized by the carefully penned bills of sale that looked so dignified compared to the impersonal tiny receipts punched out by computerized registers at bookstores she was accustomed to. Piper tried to picture what each establishment may have looked like just by their names and locations.

The Philadelphia Rare Books & Manuscripts Company, The Arsenal Building, Philadelphia.

Brattle Book Shop, Boston, Massachusetts.

Foster's Bookshop, Chiswick High Road, London.

Balagué Llibreria Antiquària, Barcelona, España.

Acadia Art & Rare Books, Queen Street, Toronto.

"Wow," Piper whispered. "Uncle Lonnie got around."

"You know, you could just about put yourself through any Ivy League college with his library, if you were inclined to sell even just a few of the rare ones," Mr. Greene suggested. "They're worth quite a lot."

"No way!" Piper responded. "I'm not selling a single one of these books."

"Why is that?" he asked.

"Well, this is how I look at it," she explained. "My uncle was a book collector, right? There's a *reason* these books were in his library. He didn't pick up those fat three-dollar paperbacks you see in drugstores near the birthday cards. He spent time and money searching for these *particular* books, and they meant something to him."

Mr. Greene smiled and said, "Your passion for books runs in the family."

Piper read every receipt in the "C" pocket, thoroughly scanning the front and back of each paper several times looking for "Cognivit."

"Not a Nemo in the bunch," she said, peering down into the empty pocket of the leather folder. Her heart dropped at the thought of how long it would take if she had to start with A and go all the way to Z to hunt for a receipt playing hide and seek.

"Oh, wait! What's this?" she asked.

A card had slipped horizontally underneath the crammed-in receipts, wedged sideways in the bottom of the bulging folder with only a tiny portion peeking out. There was just enough of the card visible for Piper to pinch the corner between her fingers and work it free without tearing it. The thick cream-colored paper was folded in half, adorned simply with "A Gift for You" in elegant black calligraphy. "To Lonnie and Beryl Bouchard" was typed across the top.

On the inside, "Best Wishes on Your Wedding Day" was printed in the same black calligraphy on the right side, and a personal message had been typed on the left.

Piper read aloud, "To the Book Collector. For When You Need Something New to Read." She glanced up at Mr. Greene. "It's signed Nemo, but it's just a typed signature; not handwritten."

"A note from the author?" Mr. Greene mused.

Piper ran her fingertips over the typed message, feeling the impressions made by an old-fashioned manual typewriter. "I'd love an old typewriter that writes like this someday," she said. "I like how the letters look on the paper. You can actually *feel* them, like the words have become part of the page forever."

"Your aunt has a manual typewriter in her study," said Mr. Greene. "An 1896 Granville, I think. She doesn't use it anymore, but it still works."

"So, this book was a wedding gift to my aunt and uncle," Piper said.

Mr. Greene said, "Now that I think about it, the author's name is ringing a bell of some kind," he said. He glanced at the open book and read the name aloud again. "*Nemo Cognivit.*" He strode from the room. "Be right back; again!" he said over his shoulder.

Piper looked at a few more of the receipts, telling herself that she needed to travel to every single one of the bookshops her uncle had visited so many years ago.

I wonder if any of these shops are still in business.

As Piper waited, she watched Phoenix sitting in the middle of the doggie trio on the breakfast room floor. Each dog's attention was focused squarely on the boy's face, quiet and attentive. Then Quincy lifted up a paw, and Piper's mouth dropped open as Phoenix reached down to grab the paw and give it a firm handshake.

"You *are* the Dog Whisperer!" Piper said with a laugh.

A few minutes later, Mr. Greene came back into the room with a rueful smile on his face. "This just gets stranger every day," he said.

"How's that?" Piper asked.

"It looked to me like the name was in Latin, and that would make sense, because the title of the book is in Latin," he explained. "Since you and I boxed up the Latin dictionary already, I asked your aunt to translate the name on her computer. The correspondence your aunt sends for her charity work sometimes has to be translated, and she has some good software," he explained.

"That's cool," Piper said.

He picked me up and puzzled over my spine and cover for several long seconds, shaking his head.

"So, what does it mean?" Piper asked impatiently.

He smiled. "No one knows."

"No one knows what it means?" she echoed. "I thought you just translated it."

"I mean that the literal translation of 'Nemo Cognivit' from the Latin means those exact words. *No. One. Knows.* Very clever," he mused.

Piper rolled her eyes in a huff.

"That's not funny."

30

The Impostors Arrive

We listen to the stories, the raw truth imparted
by tribe and fire, the tales of our forebears
passed down face to face, mouth to mouth,
eye to eye. This is how we know who we are.
—Anji Kusugak

M *row?*
Meh-rooooorw?
Meeeeh-rooooooorw?

Piper opened her eyes the next Saturday morning to the persistent sound of a cat meowing beneath her bedroom window. She hurried downstairs in her pajamas and opened the front door.

Mr. Mistoffelees sat on the stone steps next to the lifeless body of a large field mouse. The sleek black cat looked up and asked, *"Meh-rorw?"*

"You've brought us a present!" Piper said, crouching down to scratch the cat's ears and trying to ignore the dead rodent lying inches from her foot. Mr. Mistoffelees purred loudly, obviously pleased with his catch. He leaned into Piper's scratching fingers and then maneuvered around so that she was scratching his back. "Oh, you like that?" she asked.

A white delivery truck rumbled up the driveway. Mr. Mistoffelees shot off like a bullet and disappeared around the corner of the house, forgetting his mouse. "Carrington Designs" was printed in swirling black letters on the side of the truck.

Mr. Greene appeared at Piper's side. "Good morning, Piper," he said. "AH!" he cried, looking down at his foot.

Piper could see two mouse feet and the end of a tail sticking out from under the butler's polished dress shoe, and she laughed as Mr. Greene jumped back a few inches. "Mr. Mistoffelees is earning his keep," she said. "I'm sticking with that name, by the way. He's a loner, and black, and quiet, and small, just like Mr. Mistoffelees in the *Old Possum's Book*."

Mr. Greene nodded with an approving smile and said, "It suits him."

Piper looked toward the approaching truck. "The new library stuff, I guess?"

Mr. Greene produced a latex glove from his pocket, pulled it onto his hand, and delicately picked up the dead mouse by its tail. "That would be correct," he answered. "I'll be back in a jiffy."

Aunt Beryl came outside just then "Good morning, Piper" she said, her eyes following the box truck as it came to a stop in front of the house.

"Can I help today?" Piper asked. "With the library, I mean. I'm happy to help shelve books or whatever. I'm really good at it."

Aunt Beryl's mouth dropped open in surprise, and though she didn't exactly smile, the sharp edge of her voice became softer. "That's very kind of you to offer," she said. "But Miss Carrington has brought a crew with her for the installation, and it will be too crowded for anyone else to be in there."

Piper couldn't hide her disappointment, but she shrugged like it didn't matter and said, "That's okay." She turned to go back inside when Aunt Beryl stopped her with a hand on her arm.

"You may sit in one of the reading chairs and watch, if you like," she said. "But promise me that you won't get in anyone's way."

Piper hugged Aunt Beryl quickly, not caring that her aunt recoiled a little bit. "I promise! Thank you!" She hurried upstairs to get dressed and go find breakfast.

Phoenix was in the kitchen with a peanut butter sandwich in one hand and Gordon's photo in the other. A small dish of yogurt, fresh fruit, and crunchy granola was beside him, half empty. "Hi!" Piper said as she sat next to her brother.

Sofia brought a plate to the breakfast bar for Piper, and then came around the side and gave Piper a sideways hug. "I started reading the book you gave me last night," she said. Piper thought she saw an unshed tear bright in the corner of Sofia's eye.

"Do you like it?" Piper asked, her eager voice just above a whisper.

She nodded, confusion and gratitude mingling on her face. "It's easy to read, but . . ." She cast about for the words to express her feelings and looked at Piper with a quizzical expression. "It's not a . . . *normal* book, is it?

"Not at all!" Piper said with a wide smile. "Probably the most unusual book I have ever read in my life. Did you finish it already?"

Sofia waved her off and laughed, returning to the sink. "No, no, it's way too long! I don't read very fast at all, but I will read some more tonight." She turned once more to face Piper with a wide-eyed smile as she said, "You know, there hasn't been a *single* letter that looked backwards or faced the wrong way or jumped out of place. I haven't had to re-read a single sentence, even once! That's *never* happened before!"

Piper stared at Sofia for several seconds and then whispered, "That's awesome!"

Phoenix took the dogs outside to play after breakfast. The unloading of the Carrington delivery truck had already begun in earnest by the time Piper had finished eating. Careful not to get in anyone's way, Piper went around through the Halls of Moria and entered the Verboten Library from the other entrance. All three side tables and each of the six overstuffed chairs had been pushed into the center of the room and covered with a drop cloth. Piper quietly uncovered one of the chairs and sat with her legs tucked underneath. Thirty boxes were stacked nearby, twenty of which were labeled "Books by the Inch—When the Words Don't Matter." The last ten boxes were smaller, and these were stamped with "Beguiling Bookshelf, Ltd." Beneath the business label in small print it said "Makers of the Finest False Books Since 1981."

Piper heard high heels clacking through the foyer. Ashley Carrington of Carrington Designs came into the Verboten Library with a grimace and a clipboard and a harsh, nasally voice. "The boxes are numbered according to section and shelf order," she barked. "The longest section in the center here between the two windows is section one. The matching unit across from it is section two. The corner built-ins are three and four toward the ballroom, five and six toward the parlor. Sections one and two each have subsections marked A, B, C, and D top to bottom; do not mix them up."

The three coverall-clad workers immediately followed the woman's orders, and it was obvious to Piper that they had done this before. The men worked as a rapid-fire team as they divvied up the boxes and placed them in front of the empty shelves as instructed.

Ashley Carrington of Carrington Designs consulted her clipboard and said, "Bruce, I'll have you start on section one, top right corner. Jamal, you can start on section two; top right corner." The two men produced box-cutters from their pockets and got to work straight away. "Eddie, you can go ahead with the glue and start prepping the panels for section three."

Why do you need glue?

Glue makes me nervous, Dear Reader; very nervous, depending upon who wields it. In the hands of a book-binder, it's akin to having a broken arm set. In the hands of a toddler, it's akin to being accosted by a cement truck.

Piper realized that if she simply sat still and watched, her questions about "glue" and "false books" would be answered. Ashley Carrington of Carrington Designs wrestled one of the huge windows open as the sharp odor of strong epoxy began to permeate the room. Eddie opened one of the *Beguiling Bookshelf* boxes. When he brought out the contents, Piper's heart leapt into her throat in disbelief.

Eddie held a two-foot length of connected book spines made of beautifully decorated charcoal-gray leather, a solid panel that was ten inches tall and one inch thick. When glued to a wooden stand and placed correctly on the shelf, the result gave the illusion of a set of ten genuine leather-bound books. If she hadn't seen them fastened and glued with her own eyes, she never would have known they weren't real once they were on the shelf.

Dear Reader, the travesty was more than the girl could take.

"Fake books?!" Piper cried, incredulous. "You're decorating a library with *fake* books? That's the stupi—"

A single icy glance from Ashley Carrington of Carrington Designs stopped Piper mid-sentence. The designer didn't bother to respond to Piper's comment, and she spent the rest of the day pretending the brokenhearted girl wasn't in the room.

Aunt Beryl stepped into the Verboten Library a while later and regarded the changes with approval. "I think this will suit me just fine," she said. "I believe everything is in your notes regarding the furniture placement, but if you need to consult me on the final staging, you may send Mr. Greene to fetch me. I'll be upstairs in the study."

As Piper watched the new library begin to take shape around her, she grew more and more heartsick. Eddie glued the handsome, lifeless decorations to their measured and pre-cut wooden stands, and then inserted each fake onto its assigned shelf. They were beautifully made, perfectly placed, and tragically empty.

Piper's thoughts were a whirlwind. Decorating a library with artificial books was the same to her as furnishing a living room with a piano that was missing every last string and hammer. The pianist would see the familiar shape that promised to deliver all sorts of lovely tunes and intricate melodies. I could only imagine the disappointment the musician would feel sitting down to perform a minuet and having the effort rewarded with silence.

At least the *Books by the Inch* collection included some actual books, but the subjects were of little interest to the children. Yawn-inspiring titles such as *The Psychology of Investing*, *The History of the Arborist*, and *Ledgers and Lawyers* began to take their place on the shelves. There was even a ten-volume set titled *Chronological Standards of Statistics*. Each book was identical in height to the others, and every book was wrapped in the same beautiful charcoal gray leather binding with gold embossed lettering on the spine.

True to her word, Ashley Carrington of Carrington Designs had created a perfectly tidy, perfectly symmetrical, perfectly dead library.

31

Hatching a Scheme

You cannot open a book without learning something.
– Ancient proverb

On Sunday morning, Piper opened her eyes and looked around her bedroom, feeling more at home there than ever before. After the disaster that had befallen the Verboten Library the day before, she was even more grateful for the much-loved, often-read, hand-selected books that kept her company.

She yawned and stretched under the covers, the thoughts in her head moving in a segue from seeing her books, to reading her favorite books, to reading a certain book in a tree, to the sad shell of a library downstairs, to imagining Aunt Beryl sitting and reading a boring book in the sad shell of a library downstairs.

Piper couldn't help but wonder. Would Aunt Beryl ever sit in that beautiful room and read a *real* book, giving the comfortable chairs and well-placed lamps what they cried out for?

What book would Aunt Beryl possibly be reading in there?
What if she read . . . !?
No way . . . !
. . . Just maybe?
Piper dressed and poked her head into her brother's room and found that he had already gone downstairs to breakfast. Several papers were scattered about on his nightstand, and she was curious as to what he'd been drawing lately. Piper glanced

through four pages, all depicting penciled drawings of the same tiny object.

It was a key.

The comforting aroma of coffee greeted Piper as she came down the stairs, and as soon as she stepped into the kitchen Sofia rushed over, wrapped her arms around Piper, and held her close. Several strands of wayward hair tickled Piper's cheek.

"I finished that book," Sofia whispered after a few moments, her voice breaking with emotion. "It was . . . I can't explain it! It was like the story *knew* me. And I read it so fast!" She pulled away, dabbing at a tear in her eye and smiling broadly. "You said it was unusual, but I didn't realize what you meant." She stepped over to where she had placed me on the counter and affectionately patted my front cover.

Piper nodded. "Phoenix read it first, and it was about him, and then when I read it, I read a story about me. Mr. Greene read a story about himself, and now you!"

Sofia shook her head, her eyes wide with gratitude and wonder. "That makes no sense!"

Mr. Greene came in and poured himself a cup of coffee. Noticing what Sofia was looking at, his surprised expression melted into a satisfied grin.

"Well, Sofia, I see you've joined our secret book club," he said.

Sofia laughed and said, "I wish someone could explain it!"

Mr. Greene paused with his coffee in midair and said, "Don't we all!"

Piper sat at the breakfast bar next to Phoenix. "Good morning, little brother," she said. His plate was already empty, and he was putting the finishing touches on another drawing similar to the ones in his room.

Sofia brought Piper a plate of banana-filled crepes and a huge bowl of sliced strawberries. "Sofia, you are spoiling us rotten!"

she said as she began to devour the meal. Between bites she glanced around and asked, "Where's Aunt Beryl?"

Mr. Greene sipped his coffee. "She's taking advantage of this warm weather, attacking a row of unsuspecting bushes out in the garden with the pruning shears," he said with a bemused smile. "They won't know what hit them."

Piper looked at Phoenix, appreciating the focused attention he was giving to his drawing. He looked up at his sister and smiled before going back to what he was doing.

Piper swallowed a bite of crepe and said, "So I had a thought this morning."

"Uh, oh," Mr. Greene said with a wink.

Ignoring his taunt, Piper asked, "What do you think would happen if Aunt Beryl read this book?"

Sofia dropped her spatula.

Phoenix put his pencil down.

Mr. Greene pretended not to choke on his coffee.

The room went silent as everyone looked at Piper with startled, doubtful expressions.

"I'm serious," she said. "Do you think it would have something to tell her, like it did for all of us?"

Sofia cocked her head sideways. "Well, there is definitely something . . . powerful about it," she said. "I think having her read it can only be a good thing, but you know she never, ever reads old books. Says they make her sad for some reason, so she only reads books that are brand-new."

Phoenix stood and walked from the room. Piper figured he had to go to the bathroom.

Mr. Greene sat on the barstool opposite Piper and gazed out the window for a moment. "I can only speak for myself, because I can't be inside someone else's head and claim to know how they felt after they read it." He sipped his coffee, choosing his words carefully. "It's not logical; not in the least. But it does have some sort of . . . *power*. I can't explain it. But I would think that a magic book doesn't care who reads it. The magic lives within its pages, and the words will still be able to reach inside and change the reader. I imagine that very few people would be immune to it."

"Exactly!" said Piper. "Remember when you told me about thin places, about the tree at the edge of the garden?" she asked. "I think this book is sort of like that somehow."

Mr. Greene nodded. "I suppose *magic* is the wrong word to use, because it's not wands and spells and potions and controlling inanimate objects," he said. "It's closer to the Deep Magic that C. S. Lewis writes about in *Narnia*."

Piper nodded eagerly. "I remember that! The Deep Magic is what helped defeat the White Witch."

"Exactly," said Mr. Greene. "So this book somehow connects the reader to that same Deep Magic, like a portable thin place that brings you closer to God."

Piper said, "Sofia, if you could pick one word to say how the book made you feel after you read it, what would you say?"

I must say, Dear Reader, that asking for a single word to describe what I do is preposterous.

Sofia leaned against the kitchen sink, looking up to the ceiling as she searched for a word. She started and stopped several times, finally nodding her head with satisfaction as she said, "Worthy."

Mr. Greene took a deep breath and gazed into his coffee for a moment before he nodded and whispered, "That's a good word."

He took another sip of coffee and cleared his throat. "What about you, Piper?" he asked. "What word comes to mind?"

"Fearless," Piper said without hesitation. There were a few other words that would have also fit, but that was the word she kept returning to every time she thought about the story I had told her.

Piper stuffed another bite of crepe into her mouth. "Your turn," she countered.

"One word?" Mr. Greene asked, smiling. Then he looked up to the ceiling and said, "I suppose if I'm only allowed one word, then it would be . . . valuable."

Phoenix came back into the kitchen carrying a book under his arm. He sat on the barstool beside Piper with the book in his lap.

"Okay, so back to my suggestion," Piper said. "You felt valuable. Sofia felt worthy. I felt fearless. What would happen if Aunt Beryl read the book too? I'm sure there is something that she needs, some sort of feeling that would, I don't know, be good for her to have."

The group sat and looked at one another for a few long seconds, none of them able to verbalize what Aunt Beryl might need. Piper said, "Phoenix, we're talking about how the book made us feel. Can you tell me what you felt when you read it?"

He picked up the pencil from the counter, flipped his drawing paper over to the blank side, and wrote a single word in messy capital letters.

PHOENIX.

Piper's vision became obscured with tears. She nodded and leaned forward to give her brother a quick hug. "Yes! You felt Phoenix!"

"Holy smokes, he wrote his name!" Sofia whispered.

Mr. Greene laughed softly, shaking his head. "Unbelievable. Okay, then. I think we all agree that your aunt should read it. Now the question is, how do we convince her?"

Phoenix brought out the book that was hidden in his lap and put it on the table.

"What is this?" Piper asked.

Mr. Greene cocked an eyebrow at Phoenix and replied, "This is the new release that came in yesterday's mail. Your aunt opened the package and set the book on her nightstand to read, but there's no bookmark in it. She always uses the same leather marker with tassels on the bottom, so she hasn't started reading it yet."

Phoenix removed the glossy dust cover from the brand new book and wrapped it around me like a snug new jacket. Then he slid the newly wrapped old book toward Mr. Greene.

"Brilliant!" said Mr. Greene as his face lit up, giving Phoenix a wide smile. "Magic story, incognito."

32

Bamboozled

I'm not entirely certain they were prepared for what Story had to tell them. But Story knew it had been sent to destroy life as they knew it.
−Jameson Cooke

I'll do it!" Piper said as she jumped up from the barstool. "I'll make the switch. You said she's outside hacking up the bushes, so she won't be back inside for a while." Without waiting for a response from anyone, she took me into her arms and ran upstairs to Aunt Beryl's bedroom.

Piper had only been in Aunt Beryl's chambers once, in the dark, and she'd been too focused on the sleepwalking incident to notice much. Here in the daylight, the room's sheer size made the girl's head spin. Taking up the entire right sight of the house, the bedroom was as large as the Verboten Library below. A king-sized bed, two matching nightstands, three extra-large dog crates, and a duo of fat upholstered armchairs didn't begin to fill up the enormous space. A freestanding oval floor mirror stood in the corner facing down the hallway toward Piper's bedroom. She counted four closet doors.

In Piper's mind, the best features of the room were the two bench window seats inset deeply between each pair of closets. One of the bench seats faced the front of the house, and its twin faced the back. Thick upholstered cushions on the bench formed a perfect nook that begged for someone to curl up in the cozy alcove and read.

Aunt Beryl's room was just like Aunt Beryl: neat, tidy, properly decorated with matching fabrics, and chilly.

Piper reverently placed me on Aunt Beryl's nightstand, hoping I would somehow speak to her as I had spoken to the rest of them.

She needn't have worried, Dear Reader. I had longed to tell Aunt Beryl a story for decades.

Piper went from Aunt Beryl's bedroom into the adjoining study to see what it looked like in the daylight. From her previous midnight visit, she remembered the big desk and the set of upholstered chairs that she could now see were a salmon-colored velvet. Between the chairs was a round claw-foot table with an antique Tiffany lamp.

As Piper turned to leave the study, she noticed an old black typewriter sitting on the corner of Aunt Beryl's giant desk. A thick metal plate carved with a swirling label proclaimed it to be THE GRANVILLE AUTOMATIC. Piper had seen another antique machine like this at a library behind some glass, but the children had not been permitted to touch it. She ran her fingertips over the cold metal keys, smiling at how separated and awkward and stick-like they seemed. What looked to be a black typing ribbon was still in it, but it was faded to the color of ash, dried out and cracked.

How weird and fun would it be to type on that thing?

A moment later Piper rejoined the others at the breakfast bar and said, "I guess we just wait and see."

Phoenix and Piper spent almost the entire day outside with the dogs, exploring the forests that had begun to grow thick and lush with spring. Then the children helped Sofia in the herb garden. Piper raked the freshly tilled dirt smooth and tossed out the rocks and roots to make it ready for new seeds. Phoenix was content to play in the dirt and examine each rock that Piper unearthed.

Each time she thought about the "gift" she had left on Aunt Beryl's nightstand, Piper had to fight down the fear that rose in her throat.

When would she realize she had been tricked? Will she be mad that someone had obviously been in her room?

Will she even read it?

Dinner was consumed, showers were taken, and Piper sat up in bed reading *Holes* as Phoenix lounged at the end of her bed, drawing on some loose notebook paper. A few times Piper glanced at what Phoenix was working on and saw more of the same little images of keys.

"You've drawn lots of those keys," Piper said. "Maybe you could tell me what they mean some time."

He glanced up at Piper, smiled, and went back to his drawing.

Nine o'clock bedtime came and went, and Piper couldn't help but look at the clock every few minutes. "I wonder if she's reading the book?" she asked Phoenix.

At ten o'clock Piper faked a large yawn and pushed Phoenix out the door and down to his bedroom. "Time for bed, buddy," she whispered. Phoenix placed his pencil and papers on the nightstand and climbed beneath the covers. "Night!" Piper said as she closed his bedroom door. She crept back to her room and waited for thirty slow-moving minutes to make sure Phoenix didn't come back into her room.

There was a time when the Hardy Boys detective stories were the only thing that captured Piper's interest. Convinced that she knew enough about domestic espionage for a successful mission, Piper looked around her room to see what she could fashion into a makeshift spy device. The only small mirror she had was inside the lid of her little black wooden jewelry box. She pried the mirror loose from the lid with a pair of scissors and tucked it into the pocket of her robe.

Ting! Ting!

A duo of high-pitched notes jangled from the innards of the jewelry box, and at that moment Piper remembered the old wind-up music box inside that was activated by the opening of the lid. She closed the jewelry box and let out a breath, hoping no one had heard the jingling tune through her closed door.

She poked her head out the bedroom door and listened for a few long seconds, relieved to find the house dark and still. Aunt Beryl's doors were closed as usual. Piper padded in socked feet out of her bedroom and walked down the dark-ened hall toward the first entrance to Aunt Beryl's suite, the entrance she did not plan to use for her spying mission. That first door opened into a huge mirrored dressing room, which then led directly into Aunt Beryl's bedroom. Piper turned left and walked along the balcony, coming to stop in front of the closed study door.

Piper turned the doorknob to the study with painstaking silence. As expected, she found the room dark, but a faint glimmer of pale blue light shone underneath the door to Aunt Beryl's bedroom.

Yes! It's that light!

Is Aunt Beryl mad because we switched the cover and tricked her?

Piper had to know for sure, so she crept to the closed bedroom door and sat cross-legged on the carpet, trying to figure out her next move.

She lay down flat on her belly and crawled as close as she dared to Aunt Beryl's bedroom door without touching it. She slid the little mirror under the door, tilted it enough so she could look into the room, and tried to make sense of the upside-down image.

She saw the nightstand and the side of the king-sized bed. The bedside lamp was on, and Piper could see Aunt Beryl sitting propped up against the headboard. There was no mistaking the blue shimmer in the air around the bed, and Piper was suddenly filled with hope.

Smiling to herself, Piper started to pull the mirror back when she heard a low whine from the other side of the door. A wet black nose began sniffing the floor in earnest, depositing a blob of dog slobber onto the little mirror before Piper managed to yank it back.

"Quincy!" Aunt Beryl snapped. "Quiet!"

The sound of urgent footsteps in Aunt Beryl's bedroom met Piper's ears. Without hesitation, Piper shimmied on knees and elbows to a spot behind the massive desk. Aunt Beryl wrenched the door open, and the lamplight illuminated the space Piper had occupied just seconds earlier. The light spilling into the study was millimeters from Piper's big toe. She held her breath, hoping Quincy didn't squeeze past Aunt Beryl's leg and give away her position.

"See?!" Aunt Beryl said. "No one is there, Quincy, now back in your bed!"

Quincy responded with a disbelieving whine as Aunt Beryl closed the door. Shaking with relief, Piper tiptoed as fast as she could back into her bedroom.

Sleep did not come easily for Piper that night. She kept playing out different scenarios in her head of what might happen the next morning if Aunt Beryl had indeed read the book.

Phoenix and I are arrested for trespassing and Mr. Greene is fired for allowing someone into Aunt Beryl's bedroom.

Mr. Greene can never find work again, so he becomes a homeless beggar and wanders around town with a shopping cart.

Sofia is fired, I become the "before" version of Cinderella, and Phoenix is sent to live somewhere awful with concrete walls and never allowed to walk outside with his face to the sun.

Perhaps.

Perhaps not.

Piper heard Mr. Greene's voice echo in her thoughts just before she finally gave in to sleep.

"I would think that a magic book doesn't care who reads it. The magic lives within its pages, and the words will still be able to reach inside and change the reader. I imagine that very few people would be immune to it."

33

The Atmosphere Shifts

Brave ships are these that bear thee home again.
–Charles Hamilton Musgrove

The sunlight is brilliant in the first part of this chapter, Dear Reader. Shade your eyes if you must.

Gordon Guthrie was dreaming.

He walked along the beach just as the yellow-orange rays of a glorious dawn spilled over the azure sea. He turned toward the warmth, closing his eyes and inhaling deeply as a salty breeze touched his face. All traces of his injuries were gone, and the blood running through his veins pulsed with more life than ever before.

Gordon could see Phoenix walking toward him from far down the beach. He marveled at how much older his son looked now than when he had last seen him. The pudgy baby fat around the boy's cheeks was gone, and his light-brown hair had grown dark and thick, becoming much more like Gordon's. It was like seeing a snapshot of himself, a photo taken thirty years earlier that had come alive and was coming toward him in the sand.

Gordon had not understood when Phoenix had gradually stopped talking so many years ago; no one did. But he loved his son with a ferocity that defied explanation, and no diagnosis or label would change that. His heart swelled with tenderness and pride as his son approached.

Phoenix stopped walking, looked out toward the water, and pointed.

Gordon looked out to where Phoenix was pointing, and he saw a yellow life raft far in the distance. Squinting his eyes, he could barely make out the single flaxen-haired passenger within as the raft began pitching and bobbing up and down on a sea that grew increasingly rough and angry. Before Gordon could say or do anything, Phoenix jumped into the swelling, foaming ocean, swimming powerfully toward the raft with a speed that could only happen in dreams and movies.

The boy and the raft disappeared for a moment behind a cresting wave of white surf. When the wave subsided, Gordon's eyes flooded with tears of relief when he saw that two passengers were now in the raft. The children were straining together with a pair of oars, heading for shore, heading for him.

He reached out toward his children, yanking himself awake in his pitch-black concrete hospital room as the metal shackles clanged against the bed frame.

There was no sunlight here.

Gordon's cheeks were wet with tears.

Were you to trade places with the prisoner, Dear Reader, would this dream be like salt poured into an open wound? Or would dreams of the Light give you courage in the dark?

Something touched Gordon's shoulder in the pitch dark room, causing him to jump. It took a moment for his one open eye to adjust to the blackness, and the silhouette of the dark-eyed nurse came into focus. The inky patch of sky that Gordon could see through the tiny window told him that it was the middle of the night.

Wordlessly the nurse placed a folded stack of military-issue clothing on the grubby mattress as well as a sturdy pair of thick-soled hiking boots. Then she took Gordon's hand and pressed something small into his palm and shuffled out of the room, closing the door behind her without a sound.

In the darkness it was impossible to see what she had given him, so he turned the tiny object over and over in his hand, exploring it with his fingertips until he understood what he was holding.

It was a key.

He clenched the key between his teeth, grasping in the dark to find the lock on the shackles with his free hand and moving slowly so the metal-on-metal didn't rattle.

Found it!

In the pitch black of the room he fumbled awkwardly with one hand, but he managed to unlock the shackles and free himself from the bed frame without making a sound. As he cast the grungy hospital gown aside and felt for the clean clothes from the nurse, Gordon couldn't see the tiny white butterfly regarding him from the concrete window ledge. As he used his uninjured hand and his teeth to lace up and tie the boots that were a size too small, he didn't see the butterfly as it lighted on the end of his bed in the darkness.

Where did this key come from? How did she get it?

He froze for a moment as a darker question arose in his thoughts.

What will happen to her in the morning when they realize I'm gone?

Gordon's muscles were stiff and cramped from being in the bed for so many weeks, but the adrenaline pumping through his veins was more powerful than any fatigue. He opened the door and crept out into a darkened hallway, oblivious to the white butterfly hitching a ride on his shoulder.

I didn't get a chance to thank her.

Or to find out her name.

And then, Dear Reader, he waited, listening, breathing, trusting, hoping, determined not to leave the selfless prisoner there to die after she risked her life for his. Gordon stood frozen in a pitch-black hallway for several long seconds. Then he heard the unmistakable sound of someone crying. Reaching his hands out in front of him as he took his first tentative step into the darkness, he whispered a prayer aloud. "God, show me where she is."

Holding his breath, Gordon followed the muted sounds of sobbing, and he was energized as the sound became louder with each step. His fingertips came into contact with the concrete wall at the end of the hallway, and he could feel the space to his right open up where the hallway turned. He trailed his fingertips against the wall as he walked, utterly blind, trusting that God would guide him. He found a closed door on the left and pressed his ear to the door. The crying coming from inside reminded Gordon of Naomi.

He opened the door as silently as possible, and he heard an intake of breath as she tried to stifle her sobs. He knelt on the ground and whispered into the dark room. "It's Gordon. I'm not leaving you here."

He had to strain his ears to hear the nurse's reply. "How do I know you won't abandon me in the desert? The soldiers all say that's what you Americans will do."

Gordon hoped he sounded braver than he felt. "Your life is just as valuable as mine," he whispered. "You saved my life, and I swear to you, I will not abandon you in the desert. Take my hand. I'm holding it out."

For a few moments, he thought she would refuse. Then he felt her fingertips brush against his, and she grabbed hold of his wrist with a shaky grip.

"What about your shackles?" Gordon asked.

"The guards remove them at night," she whispered. "From now on, absolute silence. I have two eyes, and you have one. Follow and do exactly as I say."

He squeezed her hand for reassurance. "I trust you. Let's go."

34

Words Come Alive

*I've left a bit of myself in every bookstore and library
I've had the pleasure of occupying.*
—Elisabeth Joyce Gott

The next morning Piper was startled from sleep by a slobbery golden retriever tongue licking her cheek.

She pulled the covers up over her face just as all eighty pounds of wiggly Lincoln jumped onto the bed. Nosing and pawing through the blankets, he managed to locate her left ear and nibbled on it with a playful whine.

"Okay, okay! I'm awake!" she said, laughing and trying to squirm away from his affection. She patted his belly and he calmed down a little, rolling onto his back with his tongue lolling out.

Then she remembered the Bamboozling of Aunt Beryl that had taken place the night before.

Piper jumped out of bed and threw on her robe and slippers and ran down the back service stairs into the kitchen with Lincoln bounding at her heels.

Sofia was in the middle of plating an omelet.

"Well?!" Piper whispered, out of breath from sprinting.

Sofia turned around with a cryptic smile. Piper thought Sofia was trying not to cry, or had just finished crying, or both.

Her stomach dropped to her knees.

Oh great! Sofia's getting sacked!

Sofia handed Piper a breakfast tray laden with a fluffy cheese omelet and two crumb-topped blueberry muffins. "Take this into the library," she whispered.

Piper's eyebrows shot up. "The *library?*" she asked. Sofia placed a fork, a napkin, and a glass of orange juice on the tray beside the plate as Piper glanced over at the empty breakfast room. "You said library," she repeated.

Mr. Greene walked into the kitchen, the expression on his face indecipherable. "The library," he repeated with a firm nod. He didn't look as though he was about to cry. He looked like he was holding back the winning answer on a game show.

"If you say so," Piper answered, certain they had both lost their minds and were sending her to meet the wrath and doom of Aunt Beryl.

There was no way Piper was going to drop a single crumb from that tray. She walked carefully down the service passage hall, through the foyer, through the high archway and left toward the Poison Ivy Parlor. She gripped the edges of the tray so tightly that her fingers began to ache. As she reached the base of the stairs, she began to hear voices.

Piper stopped in the foyer, still holding the breakfast tray and unable to see around through the Poison Ivy Parlor into the Verboten Library to know who was talking. She recognized the rise and fall of Aunt Beryl's voice, but it was softer around the edges than Piper expected. Then she heard muffled fragments of another voice, a quiet voice she couldn't make out and strained unsuccessfully to hear.

Mr. Greene and Sofia appeared at Piper's shoulder in the foyer. Piper looked at Mr. Greene. "The *library?*" she asked again.

Mr. Greene laughed outright, propelling Piper gently toward the Poison Ivy Parlor doorway. "I thought you said you were fearless, young lady," he whispered.

She squared her shoulders and thrust out her chin. "I am," she countered. She swallowed her jitters and proceeded with faked determination through the Poison Ivy Parlor and into the Verboten Library.

Aunt Beryl?

Still in her flowered nightgown with bed-tousled hair, no makeup, and fuzzy white slippers, Aunt Beryl sat in one of the overstuffed chairs with a quilt and an open book on her lap. Phoenix was still in his pajamas, halfway sitting with one of his legs draped across the armrest and the other leg on the floor as he leaned against Aunt Beryl's shoulder. Quincy and Teddy were asleep at her feet, and Lincoln padded in to join them.

Aunt Beryl was reading aloud as Phoenix looked on, and her voice had taken on a sing-songy warmth Piper had never heard before.

> "Speak to the sea, my boy, my lad.
> Sing to the bounding main.
> Call to the tide, my boy, my lad,
> To ferry thee home again.
>
> Cheer to the briny deep, my boy.
> Summon the sparkling shore.
> Turn thy face into the waves, my boy,
> To carry thee home once more.
>
> Grip the oar strong, my boy, my lad.
> Bind yourself tight to the mast.

Shout out a song, my boy, my lad,
Your ship's found its harbor at last."

A faint, raspy voice answered back, a voice that had grown rusty and hoarse for lack of use.

"At last," he whispered.

Piper's vision blurred with an onslaught of tears as years-old memories came skidding forward into her thoughts.

I know that voice!

Her stomach lurched and her heart leapt inside her chest, her throat erupting in a sob as she realized that Phoenix had spoken. A well-placed side table just inside the doorway of the library prevented the entire breakfast tray from crashing to the floor, saving the muffins, juice, and eggs from ending up on the carpet. Piper's knees went weak and she couldn't see a thing for all the tears brimming over. She leaned against the side table, setting the tray down as quietly as she could, not wanting to break the spell of whatever was happening in there.

Aunt Beryl looked up, her eyes meeting Piper's as she nodded and smiled.

Should I run over there and hug Phoenix and make a big fuss?

Should I let him see me cry?

Should I not let him see me cry?

She hadn't heard Phoenix speak in so long, but she didn't want to do the wrong thing and make him not want to talk again. Mr. Greene and Sofia came to stand beside Piper in the doorway, and Piper could feel the two of them beaming behind her.

Piper wiped the tears away with the back of her hand and lightly said, "Is this the breakfast party?"

"Good morning, Piper," Aunt Beryl said warmly.

Did aliens show up in the middle of the night and abduct the real Aunt Beryl?

"Phoenix was just showing me one of his favorite books," Aunt Beryl said, reaching to take a cup of steaming tea from the little coffee table in front of her. She patted the empty matching chair that was drawn up next to hers. "Won't you join us?" she asked.

Piper looked at Mr. Greene and Sofia with her mouth open.

Mr. Greene leaned close to Piper's ear and whispered, "You asked for magic?" Nodding toward Aunt Beryl and Phoenix, he added, "I'd say this fits the bill."

Piper carried the breakfast tray to the coffee table. She curled up in an overstuffed chair and listened to Aunt Beryl read poems aloud to Phoenix.

Eating crumb-topped blueberry muffins.

In the *library*.

35

Fessing Up

"Come in," said the book. So the children
clasped hands and skipped into the realm
where the dead may whisper to the living.
–Francis Westbrook

Careful with this chapter, Dear Reader. Watch that the briars don't jab you in the thumbs as you turn the pages.

"Here's a set of pruning shears for you," said Aunt Beryl, handing Piper a small cutting tool that looked sharp enough to split a hair in two. "And you'll need these," she added as she handed over a bottle of Elmer's white school glue and a thick pair of leather work gloves.

"Elmer's glue?" Piper asked.

She nodded and said, "For the cane borers. Follow me."

Piper was nervous when Aunt Beryl had asked her to help in the rose garden the next day. But she didn't want to say no, since her aunt had never asked to spend time with her before, and it was a gorgeous summer morning. Plus, Dear Reader, Piper realized I had shared a story with Aunt Beryl, and now her aunt seemed . . . *different*.

Aunt Beryl donned a well-worn pair of leather gloves and pulled back one of the rosebush canes to show Piper where to cut. She said, "It's almost impossible to kill these old beauties with pruning them too much. They'll re-grow new shoots from the old wood."

Piper glanced with doubt at the fat base of the rosebush she would have sworn was dead. "Really?"

Aunt Beryl pointed to a little gray eye-shaped mark on one of the stems. "This is called a bud eye, and you want to cut right above it," she said. She demonstrated by easily snipping the unwanted cane.

"Why do you need school glue?" Piper asked.

Aunt Beryl took the glue from Piper's hand and pulled up the applicator. Squeezing out a tiny drop of glue to cover the just-cut stem, she explained, "Wasps like to get in there and lay eggs, and that kills the roses. Glue keeps the wasps out and doesn't hurt the bushes. Safer and less expensive than spreading around a bunch of poison."

As she looked around at the still-dormant bushes waiting to be pruned, Piper replied, "You know, all these roses remind me of *The Secret Garden*. Did you ever read that book? This girl finds a garden surrounded by a giant wall, and the garden has been locked up for ten years. It's filled with wandering roses that have climbed up and around and pretty much taken over everything."

Aunt Beryl paused, thinking for a moment. "I remember reading that story when I was young. Isn't there an injured boy in it? Something about a wheelchair?"

Piper nodded, eager to talk about one of her all-time favorite stories. She said, "Well, the boy wasn't injured. He wasn't even really sick. He was in a wheelchair, but the girl and one of their friends convince him there is nothing wrong with him, and they help him learn how to walk again. They said it was the magic of the garden that did it."

Aunt Beryl seemed lost in thought for a few moments, snipping branches here and there and applying a tiny dab of glue to each open cut. Then she put down the shears and looked Piper straight in the eye. Where Piper feared she would see anger, there was tenderness mixed with puzzled curiosity. "Would you know anything about how a certain book came to be on my bedside table the other night?" she asked. One side of her mouth went up in a bemused smile.

Piper bit her lip. She tried to drum up a lie that might work, but she couldn't come up with anything believable. "Well," she said, "I guess you could say it all started with Phoenix. He heard the book calling to him."

"Calling to him?" she echoed, her brow arched. "What do you mean?"

"I heard it too," Piper said. "The first day we came here. I found Phoenix in the library staring at it. The book . . . I know it sounds weird, but it whispered to u—."

"Wait," she interrupted. Aunt Beryl never interrupted. "That book was in *my* library all this time?"

Piper nodded. "Smack in the center of the middle shelf, the long one between the two windows. I could never understand what the whispers were saying, but I think Phoenix did. He told me the book wanted to be read, so he borrowed it."

Aunt Beryl nodded. "Was he talking to you then? Using his voice?"

"Oh, no," Piper said. "He has this way of writing to me, sort of like secret messages I have to decode."

"Ah," Aunt Beryl said. Piper followed from bush to bush as her aunt pruned each one. She was happy just watching, eyeing the thorny stems from a safe distance. "Go on," Aunt Beryl instructed.

"So when Phoenix took the book, he read it in one night. And the next day I could tell there was something . . . *different* about him. Something different about his eyes, I guess. I don't know," Piper said. "It's like a tiny part of Phoenix that was sleeping just sort of . . . woke up."

"And what about you?" she asked. "I assume that you have also read it?"

Piper nodded, leaning against the low stone wall as Aunt Beryl pruned. "The book was . . . It's so hard to explain!" she said. "It's like it was written about me, but about a better me, a me that wasn't so confused and mad and worried about stuff. It's like the book knew what I needed to hear and told me a story about it.

"I didn't realize at first that the book was different for everybody. I read it, and it was about me, but I couldn't figure out why Phoenix would like it so much. So I asked Phoenix what it was about, and he said it was about him. That didn't make any sense at all, so I gave it to Mr. Greene to test my theory, and—"

"He said it was about him," Aunt Beryl finished, interrupting Piper for the second time that day. "And the book I read was about me," she added with a whisper. "Extraordinary."

A confused smile tugged at Aunt Beryl's lips as she shared her thoughts. "I feel the same way you do, Piper. It was a story about me, but about the person I truly *want* to be, deep down."

While Aunt Beryl worked on a few more rosebushes, Piper watched in silence. She let out a breath she didn't know she'd been holding as she realized there was almost no trace of the strained awkwardness between them.

"Whose idea was it to pull the old switch-aroo with the new dust jacket?" Aunt Beryl asked ruefully. "Very clever."

Piper laughed. "Phoenix gets the credit for that too."

Aunt Beryl paused her pruning for a moment and looked with tenderness into Piper's eyes. "Thank you," she whispered, her voice catching in her throat in an uncustomary display of emotion. "And I will have to be sure and thank Phoenix, as well."

She cleared her throat as her focus went back to the pruning. "You know," she began as they moved along to the next bush, "you mentioned *The Secret Garden* a minute ago, and that has me wondering about Phoenix."

Piper cocked her head sideways and asked, "How's that?"

"If I remember that story correctly, the boy was sick and bedridden because he was afraid of something," she said. "And when his friends helped him realize there was nothing to be afraid of, he miraculously got better. Is that right?"

"Yes," Piper responded. "The boy was afraid he was becoming a crippled hunchback, because a few grown-ups kept saying he would, but those grown-ups were wrong. The garden wasn't really magical, you know? The boy was just afraid, and his friends helped him to believe in himself enough so that he got better. I'm not sure what you mean about Phoenix, though."

"You said your brother heard the book speak to him, saying it wanted to be read. What other sorts of things does Phoenix hear?" she asked.

The memory of one of the cipher notes came back to Piper with a jolt, causing hot tears to prick at the corners of her eyes. "He knew about Mom," she whispered, staring at the grass. "A couple of days before it happened. He said she would be going into the Light, *before* the car accident happened."

Aunt Beryl nodded, grief darkening her expression for a second and then giving way to awed curiosity. "Extraordinary," she whispered. "I've heard about people with those kinds of abilities before, but never thought one of them would come to live in my house!"

The memory of another of Phoenix's cryptic messages jumped forward in Piper's thoughts. "I just remembered something else Phoenix wrote to me in one of his notes," she said. "It was right after he read the book, and I don't know what it means." Her words tumbled out in a rush. "The note said, 'found it,' and the night before Phoenix wrote that, I dreamed about Dad, and in the dream I heard Dad say the same exact thing!"

Aunt Beryl lowered her arms from pruning as she looked up to the sky, perplexed and repeating what Piper had said. "Found it." She shook her head after a few moments, looking baffled. "Found what?" she asked.

Piper shrugged and said, "I have no idea."

Aunt Beryl crossed her arms, deep in thought. "You dream about your father?" she finally asked, her voice catching in her throat.

Piper nodded. "A bunch."

Aunt Beryl pulled Piper close in an unexpected hug and whispered, "I dream about him too."

Piper buried her face into Aunt Beryl's shoulder, and her voice came out in a little squeak as she asked, "Do you think he could still be alive?"

Aunt Beryl abruptly took a step back, squared her shoulders, and cleared her throat. "I would have said no a few months ago," she said. "But with everything that's happened here lately, I must admit that I'm starting to hope again, my dear."

She glanced at her watch, then put her arm around Piper's shoulder and began leading her toward the house. "I believe I have an appointment with Phoenix in the library," she said. "The roses can wait."

36

The Man at the Door

Weeping may tarry for the night,
but joy comes with the morning.
—Psalm 30:5 ESV

A week later, a crisp sunrise found Aunt Beryl seated in the Poison Ivy Parlor. She looked less than comfortable in one of the stiff upholstered chairs, fidgeting with a cup of tea that had gone cold hours earlier. Even though Aunt Beryl had grown far less standoffish with the children in recent weeks, Piper wasn't quite sure how to take the "new" version of her aunt. She didn't ask why Aunt Beryl was sitting in a room she normally never occupied, ignoring her tea.

The doorbell chimed, and before the sound had faded away Aunt Beryl announced, "I'll get the door."

Aunt Beryl never answered the door.

Hearing the doorbell, Piper came out of her bedroom to see who it might be and started down the main staircase with intentions of eavesdropping.

I hope it's not that Carrington lady, the Library Killer!

Phoenix was perched on the enormous staircase a few steps down from the top landing. He stared intently through the railings at the front door with his cheeks pressed against the posts.

Piper stood beside him on the stairs and leaned down and whispered, "Are you spying?"

He looked at Piper and smiled, his translucent green-and-amber eyes glittering with barely contained excitement. He passed her a little note, and then pulled the nearly ruined photo of Gordon from his pants pocket and held it tightly with both hands.

Piper unfolded the scrap of paper and read the single word aloud. "Waiting."

Piper grinned. "You wrote with words again! Good job, buddy! I'm so prou—"

Phoenix grabbed Piper's hand, pulling her firmly down to sit on the stair beside him.

"Okay. I guess I'm waiting with you," she said. Her voice dropped to a whisper as she asked, "What are we waiting for?"

Aunt Beryl was dressed like she was prepared to meet the Queen of England. Her hair and makeup showed that she'd taken extra care with them that morning, and her tailored yellow suit reminded Piper of something out of a magazine. Aunt Beryl smoothed down some non-existent wrinkles in her skirt, took a deep breath, and opened the front door.

Piper's limited view of the foyer and the entryway was blocked by Aunt Beryl's body, and Piper couldn't see who was on the other side of the open front door. After a few seconds of silence Piper heard Aunt Beryl's voice, shaky and thick with emotion. "I dreamed last night that you would come."

At the exact same moment, Phoenix let go of the old photograph as he uttered a faint and reverent whisper. "Daddy."

When Piper looked back on that moment much later, she couldn't remember running headlong down the stairs with Phoenix and crashing into their father as he knelt to embrace them both in the foyer. Piper could tell from the look on his face that he hurt somewhere, but Gordon tried not to show it as the children grabbed and touched and hugged and held on to as much of him as they could. His right eye was covered with a thick gauze bandage, and his right arm and shoulder were immobilized in a black cast-like contraption that bound his arm against his torso. Gordon's face was painfully thin, and it looked like he hadn't come anywhere near a razor during his entire time away.

Oh, Dear Reader, the joyous reunion in the foyer made every last letter within my pages sing!

Piper couldn't stop crying and laughing.

Gordon couldn't stop laughing and crying.

Aunt Beryl tried to pretend she wasn't crying, but she kept dabbing at her eyes with a lacy handkerchief and shaking her head in shock as she said, "I still don't believe it."

Phoenix wrapped both arms around Gordon's neck and refused to let go, smiling so wide that Piper thought her brother's cheeks would burst open. He whispered a single hoarse word over and over. "Daddy. Daddy. Daddy."

Disbelief and joy blended together on Gordon's face as he listened to Phoenix speak, and he looked at Piper, eyes wide with awe. "When?" he asked.

Piper could hardly form words as she tried to wipe the still-falling tears from her cheeks. "A couple weeks ago," she whispered.

Mr. Greene stepped into the foyer and announced, "Allow me to take your bags to your room, Mr. Guthrie." He carried himself in his usual, proper, butler-y fashion as he grinned from ear to ear.

"Thank you," was all Gordon could manage. He didn't care that he was sobbing almost uncontrollably; none of them did. With Phoenix still wrapped around him, Gordon stood up, straining under the effort but managing to keep his balance.

"You're both so *tall*!" Gordon whispered, pressing his cheek again his son's. "You two are the most beautiful things I have ever seen," he said, choking down another sob. "Piper I wish both my arms worked so I could carry you both around at the same time."

Piper didn't want to get tears and snot all over her father's injured arm, so she just smiled and shook her head. "It's okay, Dad," she said, wiping her eyes with her sleeve. "I can wait my turn."

Aunt Beryl continued to dab at her eyes as she stood in the foyer with a bewildered smile. "If I weren't so happy to see you, I'd bash you in the head for not calling to say you were coming!" she said.

Gordon's eyes flashed with anger as he shook his head. "Oh, I wanted to, more than anything! The second I walked into the embassy, the State Department took me into their custody, and I was held in lock-up until they checked out my story. I begged and pleaded, and they refused; something about politics or some sensitive mission in that area; I don't know. They put me on a plane to Bangor with an escort, and the SUV that brought me here was one of theirs." Gordon's lower lip began to tremble as he whispered, "I'm so sorry, Beryl."

Mr. Greene had retrieved a small suitcase from the driver and led Gordon, Phoenix, and Piper upstairs in a slow-moving huddle. Mr. Greene ushered them all into the guest room where the windows had been opened wide to let in the fresh summer air. At some point the room had been redone with all new linens, extra pillows, and a cozy recliner.

Gordon looked around the room, amazement brightening his expression as he lowered Phoenix to the floor. "Oh, wow, this is too much!" he said.

Mr. Greene smiled. "Ms. Bouchard would like you to come down for coffee in the breakfast room, as soon as you are ready, Mr. Guthrie." He reached out and shook Gordon's hand warmly, adding, "You have two remarkable children, and you have been greatly missed. Welcome home, sir."

Gordon sank to the bed and pulled Phoenix onto his lap. With his good arm he drew Piper to his side and took turns looking at both of his children and kissing their cheeks and foreheads over and over again. "The people at the embassy told me what happened, and I'm so sorry that I wasn't here for you when Mommy died," he said, sadness filling his voice. He had no need to wipe away his tears, and he leaned back so that he could look straight into his children's eyes. "I can't imagine how hard it was for you, moving to a new place all by yourselves. I'm so proud of how brave you've been," he said. "I promise that I will *never* leave you alone again, no matter what."

"No more job where you have to go away?" Piper asked, burrowing as close as she could under his arm.

Gordon nodded. He squeezed Piper tight and kissed Phoenix on the forehead again, breathing in the sweet, familiar scent of their hair and their skin and their breath. It was a fragrance he had never forgotten. "I'm home to stay."

A tiny white butterfly hovered about the Villa Legere entryway before coming to rest on the threshold of the open front door. She opened and closed her translucent wings a few times, resting for a moment before flitting unseen into the foyer. She hovered in midair for a second, then darted upstairs and into Piper's bedroom where Aunt Beryl had returned me after our time together.

She came to rest on my shelf and told me a story about a dark-eyed nurse meeting her family at the Israeli Embassy in Berlin. Then she tapped her antenna delicately against my spine before fluttering downstairs and out the front door toward her next assignment.

Let's leave the children to enjoy their father, shall we? It wasn't simply a joyful moment, Dear Reader.

It was pure.

It was magic.

It was holy.

It was *thin*.

37

Gift Exchange

When you sell a man a book you don't
sell him just twelve ounces of paper
and ink and glue—you sell him a whole new life.
—Christopher Morley

Gordon announced, "I have presents for you!" Two unmarked brown paper packages tied with twine graced the breakfast table. One of the gifts was about the size of a library book, and the other was about the size of a board game.

Phoenix sat on Gordon's lap. The boy had hardly let Gordon out of his sight over the three days that he had been home. Phoenix finally let go long enough for Gordon to go to the bathroom and shave and shower by himself, but that was all.

The three of them sat around the breakfast table with Aunt Beryl, Sofia, and Mr. Greene. Early that morning, Mr. Greene had driven to town and picked up a big box of warm, flaky pastries from the German bakery, surprising Sofia with a morning off from cooking. The six of them had polished off the lot, and the adults had gone through an entire pot of coffee.

Phoenix stared at the packages like it was Christmas morning, and Piper laughed at her brother's barely contained excitement. "Phoenix should go first," she said. "He's about to bust a button!"

Gordon laughed and pushed the smaller package toward Piper. "Here, you hold onto this," he said. Then he pulled the larger package closer to Phoenix. "And this one is for you, kiddo. I had wanted to give you something like this for your last birthday before I went overseas," he said.

Phoenix tore through the brown paper, revealing three thick artists' sketchpads and a box of mixed charcoal pencils. He gave Gordon a quick hug, nuzzling his dad's cheek with his own. Gordon opened the pack of already sharpened pencils, and Phoenix studied them closely for a few long moments before deciding on the one he wanted to use first. He flipped open the cover of the top tablet and started to draw with his tongue stuck out in concentration, still sitting in Gordon's lap.

With twinkling eyes, Gordon grinned and said, "You're next, Pipe."

Piper removed the twine first, then unfolded the brown paper to reveal a rustic diary bound in soft leather the color of butterscotch. "Oh, it's so pretty!" Piper breathed as she unwound the straps and opened the journal. "I've always wanted one of these!"

Gordon grinned and said, "I remember you asking for a diary for Christmas, and I didn't get the chance to get one for you before I left. Mr. Greene went on a little shopping trip for me yesterday," he explained. "We can have your name engraved on it, if you want."

Piper jumped from her chair and ran around the table to wrap her arms around Gordon's chest, mindful of his still-healing shoulder. "I love it," she whispered into his neck, breathing in the warm coffee morning scent she had missed so much.

Aunt Beryl rose from her seat with a smile and said, "Not to steal your thunder, Gordon, but I also have a gift." She glanced up at Mr. Greene and said, "Would you mind bringing it in?"

Mr. Greene left the room with a wide grin on his face. Aunt Beryl looked at Piper and said, "Close your eyes, my dear."

"Me?" she squeaked. Piper looked at Phoenix, who was engrossed in drawing with his tongue still stuck out. She glanced at Gordon, who looked as surprised as Piper felt.

"Don't look at me!" Gordon said.

Piper sat back down in her chair and closed her eyes, and she heard Mr. Greene return to the breakfast room a minute later. An object was placed on the table in front of her with a heavy-sounding thud.

"Now?" she asked.

Aunt Beryl's voice was warmed by a smile as she said, "Now."

Piper opened her eyes, grinning as she recognized the antique typewriter from Aunt Beryl's study.

"No way!" Piper whispered. She ran her fingertips across the metal keys and looked at Aunt Beryl in shock. "For *me*?"

Aunt Beryl nodded firmly. "I believe that nothing should go to waste, be it things or talent. It was a souvenir your uncle picked up on one of his book-buying trips to Europe, but I never had any use for it. Also . . ." She reached under the table and drew out an unopened ream of typing paper. "You spend so much of your time with your nose stuck in a book, I thought perhaps you had it in you to write a story or two of your own."

Ignoring the No Running in the House rule, Piper flew out of her chair toward Aunt Beryl and flung her arms around her in a tight hug. Piper breathed in, enjoying the faint mixture of lilac-scented perfume mingled with talcum powder. "Thank you!" she said.

Aunt Beryl patted Piper on the back. "It's a gift for the both of you," she said, nodding toward the still-drawing Phoenix. "One day he might like to type on it as well."

Piper went back to her seat to examine the gift more closely. "Is that a new typing ribbon thingy in there?" she asked.

Aunt Beryl dipped her head toward Mr. Greene as she said, "Thank Mr. Greene for finding it on the internet for me. I was surprised to learn you can't just pick them up at the corner store any longer."

Mr. Greene smiled, raising his coffee cup toward Piper in the air as he said, "Dibs on reading your first draft."

"I know you have a laptop you can write on," Aunt Beryl said. She patted the typewriter and said, "But writing on something like this is . . . *different.*"

"I know!" Piper gushed. "Smashing the ink into the paper makes whatever you're writing seem more alive or something."

Gordon said, "We'll rustle up a proper desk to go in your room so you can write whenever you like."

Piper looked around the table, her heart swelling as her eyes went from Mr. Greene to Sofia to Aunt Beryl to her dad to Phoenix.

This house is finally starting to feel like home.

38

Freedom House

Just thinking about being chained in one place forever makes my ink dry up. If I were chained to a library desk, I could never venture into the homes of my Readers and cozy up to a roaring fire in a bleak midwinter.
—Bestil Haruldane

The car pulled up to the curb and stopped in front of a pleasant drive sheltered by trees. "Is this where we turn?" Piper asked, leaning to look out the window. She read the sign aloud. "Waterville Community Complex, next right."

Mr. Greene nodded. "This is it," he said. The trip from Côte de Gris to Waterville had taken a little less than two hours.

Mr. Greene and Piper could have made the trip alone, but Gordon insisted on the four of them going together. Gordon and Phoenix were sitting beside Piper in the spacious back seat, and Phoenix had fallen asleep an hour earlier.

"We're here, buddy," Gordon whispered, stroking Phoenix's hair. Phoenix sat up and blinked, looking out the car window with interest.

Gordon had reunited with his family six weeks earlier, and the gaunt look in his cheeks was just a memory now. With Sofia's delicious meals, and with daily walks in the sunshine with

Piper and Phoenix, Gordon was looking much more like his old self again. He had exchanged the gauze bandage for a sleek leather eye patch a few weeks earlier, but his arm and shoulder remained immobile in the sling while they continued to heal after a second surgery.

"So this is the place you picked?" Mr. Greene asked, looking over the grounds with an approving nod. "I think every library should have at least one magic book on the shelf."

Mr. Greene turned the car into the entrance and drove through the grounds, passing several weathered buildings with signs like, "Head Start," and "Job Assistance," and "Community Food Pantry." He drove toward the back of the complex, and the driveway circled around in front of a stately brick building that appeared to have stepped out of an 1800's photograph. Two stories tall, the brick-red building was designed in the New England colonial fashion with tall chimneys on both sides, a steeply pitched tin roof, and a welcoming front porch. A hand-lettered sign proclaimed FREEDOM HOUSE LIBRARY.

Mr. Greene brought the car to a stop, and all four travelers climbed out to stretch their legs. Part of Piper grieved my going away, but she also knew it was time.

I knew it as well, Dear Reader. I was created to be shared, to be given away to the next person who needed me. Piper's heart was far too large to keep me to herself.

She led the group up the stairs and into the library through an imposing set of double doors. The interior of the building had also retained its 1800's-era décor.

Do you smell that, Dear Reader? It's the scent of ink, paper, dust, time, and *Story*. Breathe it in. Put the wide-open spine to your nose, and inhale. No matter if someone is watching.

Piper was glad to find the library stocked with plenty of modern books, a bank of computers, and desks for studying in various corners. A smiling young librarian sat behind an antique round circulation desk. "Do you need help finding something today?" she asked.

"I called a week ago about a book donation," Piper said. Gordon, Phoenix, and Mr. Greene began to browse among the stacks and tables. Piper ran her fingers across my front cover one more time, then slid the book across the desk to the librarian with a determined nod. "Did I talk to you on the phone?"

The librarian's face lit up. "Oh, yes! I'm Tammy. I believe we did speak on the phone. Lovely to meet you, my dear." She pulled a pen from a nearby drawer and said, "When a book is donated, we like to make a dedication sticker that goes inside the front cover, saying who the book was donated by with a few words of thanks. What name would you like to be listed?"

Piper thought hard about her answer, going from her name to Aunt Beryl to her dad, Phoenix, and Naomi, but none of them felt right. Looking at the cover again, Piper smiled as another name came to mind. "I'd like for it to say, 'Courtesy of Uncle Lonnie's Library.'"

Tammy penned the dedication in neat, swirly handwriting and held the label up for Piper's approval. "Does this look right?" she asked.

"It's perfect," Piper said.

Tammy carefully placed the sticker inside my front cover. Then she taped on a spine label and fastened a library card pocket inside my back cover, complete with a blank due-date card. "I had the card pocket and a spine label typed up right after you called," Tammy explained. "We're switching over to the barcode system next year, but now this guy is all ready to check out." Tammy reached out to shake Piper's hand. "The

Freedom House Library thanks you for your donation, young lady," she said. "You're welcome to look around if you like."

I was left there on the counter unattended. Tammy pushed a book-laden cart into the stacks on the other side of the room and began shelving the day's returns.

It was hard to turn down time at a library, but Piper wasn't inclined to browse at the moment. As the four of them gathered near the front door, Phoenix's stomach growled long and loud. Gordon tousled his son's hair with a grin and said, "Let's go find someplace wonderful to stuff our faces and feed this boy." Then Gordon cupped Piper's cheek with his hand and said, "I am so proud of you, Piper. I know how much you cherish your books, and it's very mature and thoughtful of you to donate one." He leaned forward to kiss her forehead, and Piper breathed in his aroma: peppermint, with a hint of strong coffee.

Piper looked up into Gordon's eyes, barely suppressing a pout. "I still don't understand why you couldn't read it. I thought for sure you needed a story all your own too," she said.

Does it surprise you, Dear Reader, that I did not have a story to tell Gordon? I don't have a ready answer, I must admit. I'm at the mercy of my Creator and can only deliver the stories that well up inside my pages. I do not create them.

Gordon hugged Piper with his good arm and knelt down in front of her. With a shrug he said, "What can I say, Pipe? The pages of the book you gave me were blank." He kissed her forehead and added, "God has given me *everything* I need right here, and we have enough stories between the three of us to last a lifetime."

Phoenix took Piper's hand, Piper took Gordon's hand, and the trio headed toward the exit with Mr. Greene.

Just before the big doors began to close behind them, a girl about Piper's age brushed past the Guthrie family and into the library, glaring at her shoes as she went. "I'll be just a second, Dad," Piper said as she dropped back to hold the door open for the girl.

As Piper recognized a familiar sadness in the girl's face, her heart began to ache. Piper lingered in the doorway for a moment, watching. The girl drifted aimlessly through the shelves, trailing her fingers on spine after spine in a half-hearted search for something to read.

My spine began to tingle. (How I *do* love this part!)

The girl paused. She cocked her head sideways as curiosity and confusion toyed with her features.

Piper's heart skipped a beat as she watched from the doorway.

The girl closed her eyes and became absolutely still, her brows furrowing as she tucked a wayward coil of dark hair behind one ear and turned her head.

She's listening!

After several moments her solemn expression lit up with intrigue as she made a beeline for the circulation desk. A pale blue light shimmered in the air, and the girl blinked.

Hello, Dearest Sasha. I am honored to know you.

Sasha picked me up from where I had just been placed and ran her fingers over my worn front cover, turning me over to gaze at my spine. Better than anyone, Piper understood the puzzled smile on Sasha's face as she looked from left to right, searching the deserted library with a confused gaze.

Piper slipped out the front door, and it closed behind her with a solid thump.

39

A Final Mysterious Message

The story wanted to be written, so it worried and prodded and pestered the poor girl until she gave it flesh and blood in the form of ink on paper.
−Eunice Sprague

Piper's bedroom had been turned into her own personalized writer's study. The aroma of a cinnamon-scented candle mingled with the scent of peppermint tea. The dark spool of a fresh typewriter ribbon and a new ream of paper filled Piper's belly with anticipation.

The desk Mr. Greene rescued from the basement fit perfectly in the corner of Piper's room near one of the windows. Aunt Beryl had showed Piper how the clumsy ribbon was inserted into the machine, and Piper was required to practice taking the spools in and out for when she would need to replace them on her own. Aunt Beryl also watched Piper roll the paper in and out a few times so that she got the hang of putting it in straight. Going from tablets, palm-sized cellphones, and two-inch USB jump drives to this bulky relic was so strange to Piper that she couldn't help but laugh. Twice she caught herself looking for a nonexistent power switch.

Piper donned her comfy slippers and took a sip of peppermint tea. She inserted a blank sheet of paper into the typewriter and managed to get it jammed underneath the roller. Afraid of tearing the paper and leaving bits of it under the roller, she felt around the edges of the machine for some sort of latch that would let her open the giant metal contraption. The top half was fastened to the bottom half with four tiny screws.

Mr. Greene had showed Piper where the small tools were kept in the basement, so in no time she retrieved a little screwdriver and began working the screws loose. They were shallow and turned easily, and it took just a few minutes to remove the lid and extract the wedged-in paper.

As Piper went to replace the heavy top, she noticed a small brass plate welded to the inside of the lid, an inch-tall metal rectangle bearing an engraved inscription.

To the Book Collector.
FOR WHEN A NEW STORY WANTS TO BE
WRITTEN.
MAY OUR STORIES BE TOLD,
AND MAY THE WORDS HAVE LIFE.
N.C.

Piper ran her fingers over the engraving. She remembered that, according to Aunt Beryl, Uncle Lonnie had brought the antique contraption back with him from a trip to Europe many years ago.

I'd bet a hundred bucks that it's our own Nemo Cognivit!

With intentions of showing the new discovery to her family later, Piper hoisted the lid into place and put the screws back in. Making sure the edges of her paper were straight this time, she successfully rolled a fresh sheet down to where she thought the first word should begin and stared at the empty page. Thinking about what kind of story she wanted to write, she wrapped her hands around the cup of tea, her thoughts bouncing around and bumping into memories to see if they had the makings of a good story. She glanced up at the bookshelf and her eyes landed on a beloved children's book Mr. Greene had commented on the day he helped Piper unpack. Piper's favorite line from that book-centric tale echoed inside her head in Mr. Greene's resonating voice.

"Everyone's story matters."

As Piper stared at the spine of the children's book on the shelf and repeated that sentence in her head, she began to hear a series of clicks and clacks coming from the typewriter. When she looked down at the paper, she saw a sentence printed there.

She hadn't touched a key.

She still had both hands wrapped around her cup.

With shaking fingers, she set her tea beside the typewriter and rolled the paper up to see what it said.

`Everyone's story matters.`

A Note from
Novus Fabula

Dear Reader, several of the delightful quotes I've included to start these chapters are from dear book friends of mine. But sadly, these fellow books are not to be found on typical human library shelves. They belong to my world only; yet I'm thrilled to have shared a few of their lovely words with you.

There are a few quotes whose words are pulled from books that are indeed found on your world's shelves. I have listed those below for you. Ask a librarian if you need help finding them. He or she might just have another extremely special book for you to read as well. . . .

Page 25   The Christian Standard Bible

Page 72   New Revised Standard Version Bible

Page 108   Holy Bible, New International Version

Page 130   Francis Bacon, from "Of Studies," in *Complete Essays* (Mineola, NY: Dover Publications, 2008), 150.

Page 139   Holy Bible, New King James Version

Page 180   Ancient proverb. Public domain.

Page 192   Charles Hamilton Musgrove, from "The Admiral's Return," in *Pan and Aeolus: Poems* (Louisville, KY: John P. Morton, 1913), 25.

Page 208   The Holy Bible, English Standard Version

Page 214   Christopher Morley, *Parnassus on Wheels* (Garden City, NY: Doubleday, Page, and Company, 1917), 39.

Acknowledgments

To my agent, Elizabeth Bennett: Thank you for believing in a newbie. I cried the day you called me with an offer for representation. This is just the beginning.

To the entire B&H team: You're amazing! Working with Michelle Prater Freeman, Anna Sargeant, Amanda Mae Steele, Jenaye White, and Mary Wiley has been wonderful, and there are many others whose names I don't know. It truly takes a village, and I'm honored to know you all.

To the book launch crew around the world: Thank you for helping me achieve so much! I couldn't have done it without your mad skills on the interwebs.

To Talitha Seibel: WOW! Your encouragement and constructive feedback were invaluable for making this book all it could be.

To my beta readers: Madison Agans, Kathleen Ball, Bernadette Golitz, Prisca Hill, Cheryl Lewis, Faith Mire, Laurel Phillips, Selah Seibel, Talitha Seibel, Sarah Stewart, Noël Roberds, and Tammy West. Thank you for giving me the precious resource of your time.

To The Dragonfly (Collinwood, TN) and the Collinwood Public Library: Thanks for letting me use your Wi-Fi every time my DSL went down. It was down a *lot*.

To LeAnne Riggsbee: Thank you for reading all the things, and for believing I can walk on water backward in high heels.

To Joy Willow and the Shoals Writers Guild: Thank you for your wholehearted encouragement and support. I love the writing community we're all building together.

To Lucy Fowler and the Restoring the Foundations prayer team: Thank you all for listening to the Holy Spirit as you prayed for me and for this project. You touched my soul.

To my parents, Robert and Susan Fortner: Thank you for buying me my first empty notebook and my first typewriter. I finally put them to good use.

To Nanci Lamborn: You're the strongest, bestest, most prayingest twin sister I could ever have hoped for. I love you, and I think it's time for another cruise.

To Marlena, Josh, Sarah, and Jonathan: Thank you for growing up to be incredible adults. I have no doubt you will all keep me from getting weird.

To my husband Chad: I love you more every day. Thank you for walking through it all with me, and for eating frozen dinners every November since 2011 so I could do NaNoWriMo. Ireland awaits.

And finally, to Jesus: I can't thank You enough. It's all for You, and I will spend my life knowing You and making You known.

About the Author

A.S. Mackey's first foray into writing took place when she was an elementary school kid in Smyrna, Georgia. Her debut "book" was a Steno pad full of poems, given to her parents as a Christmas gift when she was eight. As a preteen, her journals overflowed with lofty, angst-filled poetry, and she wrote her first sci-fi novel at age fifteen. (It was horrid.) Her nickname in high school was Webster, but she did not, in fact, read the dictionary for fun.

Her love for creative writing was solidified with a bachelor's degree in English literature from the University of Georgia in 1991. During her senior year at UGA, she was a reporter and copy editor for the *Oglethorpe Echo* newspaper in Lexington, Georgia. From 1992 to 1993 she was a regular humor column contributor in the quarterly independent musicians' magazine *Visions of Gray*, writing under the pen name of Uncle Earl. Allison is also a musician, and she wrote and recorded an original eleven-song CD in 2003 titled *You've Waited Long Enough*.

Mrs. Mackey has written multiple children's stories on a contract basis with Tiny Readers Publishing in Houston in 2014. She has also created web content for scores of websites around the world through Upwork. She loves to cook, and a recipe she helped develop with her identical twin sister is included in the 2017 edition of *The Old Farmer's Almanac Readers' Best Recipes and the Stories Behind Them*.

She enjoys speaking to students of all ages and has taught creative writing workshops in Alabama, Georgia, and Tennessee.

Honored to be represented by agent Elizabeth Bennett at the Transatlantic Literary Agency, Mackey is also the secretary of the Shoals Writers Guild in Florence, Alabama, where she currently lives. She and her husband, Chad, are church planters and worship leaders, and she is the mother of three adult children and a son-in-law.